Molly stared at the poster on her closet door

It was from Mitch Marlow's latest film, *Dangerous*. He was dressed in leather down to his fingertips—an American rebel astride a black motorcycle. Dark sunglasses hid his crystal-blue eyes, and a day's growth of beard ghosted his lean jaw.

Just looking at his picture had her mumbling *baby, oh, baby*—and she was supposed to *baby-sit* him?

She could do this. She *had* to do this. A career opportunity like this didn't come along every day, and she wasn't about to let a little thing like sexual attraction trip her up.

She just had to find a way to reduce him to human status. But all she could come up with was the advice given to people who were nervous about speaking before large crowds.

And somehow she didn't think imagining Mitch Marlow naked was going to help....

"What do you mean, 'no'?" perhaps best personifies **Tiffany White**. This is her fifth Temptation novel—all inspired by a rejection letter she received from another publisher. She promptly quit her job to write full-time— with outrageous results! Her books are fun and sexy. And in October, Tiffany gives her own unique spin to the legend of Sir Gawain in *Naughty Talk*.

Books by Tiffany White

HARLEQUIN TEMPTATION

BAD ATTITUDE

TIFFANY WHITE

Harlequin Books

TORONTO • NEW YORK • LONDON
AMSTERDAM • PARIS • SYDNEY • HAMBURG
STOCKHOLM • ATHENS • TOKYO • MILAN
MADRID • WARSAW • BUDAPEST • AUCKLAND

For my writer friend, Sandra Canfield,
and my fire fighter friend, Linda Shoemake,
the Thelma and Louise of *Bad Attitude*

Also, special thanks to Toni Collins
for her International Intruder connection

Published May 1993

ISBN 0-373-25542-X

BAD ATTITUDE

Printed in U.S.A.

1

"GET ME A COFFEE and a loaded gun!" Peter Ketteridge demanded.

No one answered. The early-morning silence of the Ketteridge Talent Agency unnerved him. He threw the copy of the *International Intruder* onto his lacquer-topped desk, along with his extrathin, leather briefcase, and cursed. Damn! Five years of hard work as the head of his own agency and now this!

He tapped the cordless headset that was the lifeline of his business and noted the time with a glance at his vintage watch. No one was due at the agency for another half hour.

Taking off his round glasses, he unbuttoned the jacket of his broad-shouldered suit, slouched in his chair and loosened his tie, all the while glaring at the image of the blue-eyed, fair-haired, pain in the butt of a client that smiled at him from the tabloid's front page. Instead of ducking or scowling like most paparazzi-shy, sensible celebrities, Mitch had smiled directly at the camera.

Peter scanned the copy once again, hoping he'd overreacted.

He hadn't.

Dealing with creative people was a double-edged sword. It was never boring, but it was never safe. Artists often behaved like children. He understood that their ability to contact the inner child was the source of their talent. Still, too often he felt like a baby-sitter instead of an agent.

This time I'm really going to kill him.

Peter couldn't help but compare Mitch to himself. He knew he had a polished, urbane style, but had to admit that his features were nondescript. Everything he'd acquired he owed to his tremendous drive and effort, everything from success in his career to women.

His client, on the other hand, had only to wait for those same things to drop into his lap as if they were his due. Everything came too easily to him.

To be fair, Peter had to admit Mitch didn't exactly trade on his incredible charisma. Like the sun—it just was.

It was hard not to love the guy. Harder still not to hate him.

For the past five years Mitch Marlow had been the reigning heartthrob of the silver screen, fulfilling female fantasies by playing rebellious charmers. He was James Dean reborn, with a decidedly nineties spin.

Peter had practically built his agency on Mitch Marlow. In the early days the two of them had been quite a team. Now Mitch was only one of the many important clients the Ketteridge Agency represented—this year's Academy Award-Winning director, a screen-writing team responsible for a current hit television series, and a multitalented international rock star, as well as the rock star's wife, who was writing a cookbook of the band's favorite recipes.

But the agency's specialty remained the talent in front of the camera.

It had been some time since Peter involved himself with the day-to-day routine of his client's welfare. He'd learned to delegate all but the most important matters to his staff. After all, his busy schedule wouldn't allow him to personally handle the problem Mitch Marlow had become.

Peter could mark the date on the calendar the trouble had started—the day, eight months earlier, when Mitch's twin brother had been killed in a racing accident. Since then, Mitch's exploits had made him the darling of the tabloids. But there were others who whispered that Mitch Marlow was hellbent on a path of self-destruction.

On this particular morning Peter was inclined to believe they were right.

Matthew's death had put Mitch into a tailspin.

His brother's death had been the first negative in Mitch's charmed existence, the first thing he couldn't change. Couldn't, in fact, seem to get through at all.

Reaching for his date book, Peter flipped through the appointments listed for the week, then glanced around his sleek office at the movie posters, framed sheet music, signed photographs and awards, mementos of his clients' successes—and his own.

The Ketteridge Agency was a small talent agency, not quite in the top league, yet. Though he was genuinely fond of Mitch and worried that he might harm himself, Peter's first concern had to be for his business. The press Mitch was generating was not going to help Ketteridge break into the closed circle of the big four.

Until now he had indulged his client's strange method of grieving. But when Mitch started showing up in his birthday suit on the cover of a national tabloid—when it most definitely wasn't his birthday—it was time for action.

Peter knew he couldn't allow Mitch to throw away the career they had both worked so hard on. He needed to send someone to the movie set in the Midwest, someone the star couldn't charm or influence.

But whom?

Peter looked up at the sound of footsteps.

"Mr. Ketteridge, this just came for..." Molly Hill, the ambitious, second-year agent trainee who always came in early, stood in the doorway of his private office, waving an express mail envelope in her right hand.

"Where's my coffee?" he wanted to know.

"I don't do coffee."

"The loaded gun, then...?"

"It would be a violation of my parole."

If Peter Ketteridge could have done so, he would have rubbed his hands together with glee. Providence had intervened.

"Come in and sit down. Ms. Molly Hill... isn't it?" he said, smiling expansively as he took the express mail envelope from her, then propped his expensive, glove-soft leather loafers on his desk.

She took a seat, and he studied her covertly while he slid the contract from the envelope.

Unlike many of the young agent trainees, she didn't use her position at the agency to mine the pool of good-looking amateur talent for dates. Instead she showed up at industry functions, a job requirement, with men who were more brain than brawn.

Molly Hill was acerbic, ambitious and by today's standards plumpish. She just might be the right candidate for the job of rescuing Mitch Marlow from himself. She evidently liked a man who used his brain, something Mitch Marlow hadn't been doing since his twin's death.

Tossing aside the contract, Peter finally made eye contact with her.

She didn't look away, and that annoyed him slightly; she wasn't as easily intimidated as most people were. But this was a quality that would enable her to handle Mitch Marlow.

Despite the early hour, the fax machine came to life, startling both of them. Rising to take the message, Peter crossed the office and closed the door.

"Just how badly do you want to be an agent, Molly?" he asked on the way back to his seat.

Had her spine really stiffened, he wondered, or had it been his imagination?

"Excuse me?" Molly inquired, clearing her throat and crossing her arms in front of her. She shifted her body, trying to sit with some decorum in the low-slung, black leather chair, which must have been chosen for its museum-quality appearance rather than its function.

"It's a simple enough question. I have a proposition for you, Ms. Hill," Peter explained, switching back to the more formal address so she wouldn't get the wrong idea.

She waited. Silence once again surrounded them now that the fax was quiet.

"Yes...well," he continued, uncomfortable with the realization that she could unnerve him. "To put it bluntly, Ms. Hill, the agency has a client who needs to have...well, he needs to have a knot jerked in his tail."

Molly followed the direction of Peter Ketteridge's gaze to the tabloid lying on his desk. "Mitch Marlow," she said without enthusiasm.

"Exactly. He needs a keeper, and that's where you come in," Peter said, absently doodling a beard and glasses on his client's picture with his fat, black, gold-trimmed pen. He stopped in midstroke when he realized he was drawing on a loincloth, as well.

"Right," Molly said, her voice dripping sarcasm. "I'm sure Mitch Marlow is just going to allow me to waltz into his life and derail his exhilarating ride on the suicide express."

"He doesn't have any choice in the matter. The studio brass insist the agency send a keeper for the wrap of the film to protect their investment." He was certain they would be on the phone to him as soon as they saw the cover of this paper.

"You've talked with Mitch Marlow about this already, then, and he's agreed to it?" Molly asked, doubt tinging her words.

"No, but I will," Peter said, steepling his fingers and peering at her over them. "Regardless, he doesn't have any say in the matter."

"I still think I'll pass."

"Why?"

"I'm not masochistic enough to go to the Midwest *and* deal with Mitch Marlow."

Peter studied her. She was a piece of work, all right. Any other female agent would offer to pay him to "deal with" Mitch Marlow! They'd even go to the dreaded Midwest. He tapped his pen on the desk while he considered her opposition. Once again, he summoned up his expansive smile. "Suppose I sweeten the pot. . . ."

She just looked at him. "There aren't enough brownies in the world. . . ."

"How about brownie points?" he countered.

"What's the deal?" she asked, her green eyes narrow with suspicion.

"You agree to the assignment, and there's a promotion to full-fledged agent in it for you when you succeed." No matter what Mitch's reputation, Peter knew exactly how tempting his offer was. It would shave two years off her apprenticeship.

Molly slowly uncrossed her arms. "What—what is it you want me to do exactly?"

Peter swallowed his smile. Yeah, he was good, all right. Negotiating was his ball game—hell, he owned the ballpark. Little Ms. Hill was not nearly as clever as she thought. She could have gotten more.

If she handled Mitch Marlow . . . he won. If she didn't . . . he still won.

He almost wished he could be there when her ambition came up against Mitch's attitude. "In a nutshell, I want you to baby-sit Mitch. He isn't to be out of your sight until the completion of the film."

"Baby-sit him. . . ."

Peter nodded.

"The studio brass are livid, because the film is way over budget and weeks past its deadline, all due to Mitch's reckless antics. Even the insurance company is threatening to cut him loose."

Peter laid down his pen and fastened Molly with an intent stare. "Frankly, I don't care how you go about accomplishing it, Ms. Hill, but until this film is wrapped, I don't want to see Mitch Marlow's face." He glanced down and grimaced. "Nor do I want to see any other part of him on the cover of a tabloid or hear about one more hair-raising stunt. . . .Understand?"

Molly nodded.

"Can I see that?" she asked, pointing to the paper on his desk.

He pushed the trash journalism toward her.

As she tilted her head to read, the scent of fresh strawberries wafted toward him, her unruly mass of red curls swinging forward. A tiny sprinkling of freckles across the bridge of her perfect nose was noticeable only because of the paleness of her almost translucent complexion.

"Well?" he asked when she looked up from scanning the copy. "How about it? Think you can manage to turn Mitch around? I'm tired of seeing the agency's name in the tabloids."

"I can try."

"That's not good enough."

"All right, I can do it, okay?" Molly said, rolling her eyes heavenward. She stood. "I want double my current salary and my elevation to full agent status if I succeed, and I want it in writing. Oh, and don't be surprised to see a whip and chair listed on my expense account."

"Agreed," Peter said, offering her his hand.

"When do I start?" she asked.

"Right now. Go on back to your place and pack. Use your company credit card for whatever whips and chains you might happen to need."

"That's whip and chair," Molly corrected.

Peter raised an elegant eyebrow. "Indeed. Then you haven't been keeping up with the tabloids. Well, at any rate, I'll have an airplane ticket awaiting you at the counter when you arrive at the airport."

Molly nodded, moved away and was almost at the door when she hesitated, turned and asked, "Why me?"

"Because I trust you not to get involved in a physical relationship. And because I want to know just how badly you want to be an agent. Fail at this, and there won't be a second chance."

"Don't worry. I plan to make Mitch Marlow want to live."

"How do you plan to do that?"

"Massage his ego. What else?"

"See that you keep the massaging to his ego . . ." Peter mumbled beneath his breath " . . . and nothing else."

MOLLY CONSIDERED the clothing she'd pulled randomly from her closet to pack for her trip to Saint Louis.

The Midwest. Missouri, to be exact. How lucky could she get!

Didn't dragons still roam there? No matter; she wasn't their type. They preferred virgins, if she recalled her history lessons correctly.

Picking up a suitcase, she flung it onto the bed and flipped open the lock. Was Peter so sure she wasn't the type to get involved in a *merely* physical relationship just because she wasn't a size two?

Or was it because she was an ambitious career woman, unlike the blond socialite Mitch had been frolicking with on the cover of the supermarket tabloid?

Then again, there was always the little matter of her cutting wit. That got her into trouble more often than it helped her out.

Whom was she kidding? He'd been referring to her tendency to be plump. Looking at the pair of baggy jeans in her hands, she tossed them aside and packed her second-skin, Lycra separates: a paprika crop top and matching, lace-trimmed capri leggings.

She preferred the word "voluptuous."

After all, she was only ten pounds or so heavier than the weight charts in popular women's magazines recommended as ideal for her five-foot, six inch frame. Charts, she was certain, made up by sadists who hated women with curves. As far as she was concerned, any man who wanted a woman with a body harder than his own was suspect.

Her college days had been spent dieting herself into depression, trying to mold her curves into the single-digit dress size that was continually splashed across the pages of fashion magazines as the only acceptable standard.

Only in her senior year in college had she accepted she was and always would be a size twelve, and any man who didn't like it could just go . . . away.

Now Mitch Marlow's obvious taste for nubile blondes had brought back some of her old insecurity.

She shook her head, letting her mass of red curls tumble around her face, and gave herself a talking-to. She mustn't let the handsome actor's blue eyes, sexy body and charismatic smile get to her. If she gave him any advantage, he'd take it and use it to get rid of her, once she arrived on the set. One thing she was certain of. He was not going to be pleased to have a baby-sitter.

The tape she was playing began what could be Mitch's theme song—"I'm No Angel." Pushing aside a pile of undies, she sank onto the bed, losing herself in the lyrics.

Leaning back, humming along, she caught sight of the movie poster on the back of her closet door. It was from Mitch's latest film, *Dangerous*. He was dressed in leather, down to the black gloves that exposed his fingertips; an American rebel astride a gleaming black motorcycle.

A kerchief was tied, Gypsy fashion, over his golden locks, and a gold hoop pierced one ear. Dark sunglasses hid his crystal-blue eyes, while a day's growth of whiskers ghosted his lean jaw.

None of this hid his incredible sex appeal. A living life force leaped out at her, daring her. She could almost hear his husky whisper.... *Come on, baby. Come for a ride with me. I'll take you places you've never been.*

He wasn't talking scenery.

He was young, lean and raw. A rule breaker.

Her secret fantasy.

And she was going to baby-sit him.

Yeah, right.

Greg Allman finally stopped singing about the spurs that jingled, and she got up to finish packing. Peter Ketteridge had dangled the carrot, so she'd hop. She could do this. She *had* to do it.

Opportunities like this didn't come along just every day.

Really? her conscience inquired. And which opportunity was she pursuing?

Baby-sitter, indeed. It was like sending the chicken to baby-sit the fox. Just looking at his picture had her mumbling, *Baby, baby, oh baby.* He was the one movie actor who'd never failed to provoke lustful thoughts in the darkened theater.

What would his appeal be like in the flesh?

Probably the difference between a lamp that was off and one that was switched on; the difference would be measured in megawatts.

Why couldn't she be sent to ride herd on some other actor . . . any other actor? Why did it have to be the one she never tired of looking at? How was she going to hide her attraction from him?

No matter. She'd find a way.

Peter Ketteridge had promised her full-fledged agent status if she succeeded. She wasn't about to let a little thing like sex trip her up.

All the way to the airport, during the flight and the taxi ride to the filming location, she tried to come up with a way to reduce Mitch Marlow's godlike screen image to mere mortal form. All she could come up with was the advice given to people who were nervous about speaking before large crowds.

Somehow she didn't think imagining Mitch Marlow naked was going to be the right approach to take.

2

MITCH MARLOW SPRAWLED in the canvas director chair, a bad hand of poker barely holding his attention.

"You in, Mitch?" the key grip asked, after raising the pot. The makeshift poker table was set up in the clearing outside Meramec Caverns, the old James gang hideout fifty miles west of Saint Louis.

"Yeah, I'm in," he answered, tossing in a few coins and shifting uncomfortably in his chair.

The movie they were making was titled *Jesse*, and he had the lead role, playing the famous outlaw. A lot of movies had been made about the James gang, but this was the first rock Western.

The critics were hedging their bets. Had it not been for the fact that every vehicle starring Mitch Marlow had grossed big-time profits, they'd be predicting a disaster. And if Mitch Marlow could really sing, then the sky was the limit. The sound track would sell millions and feed the publicity for the movie. Mitch Marlow knew his name made the outcome of this crapshoot only a little more predictable, but in the movie business anything could happen.

Since the movie was a Western, the costume department had pulled out all the stops; leather vest and chaps, cowboy boots and hat, silver spurs, and a pearl-handled revolver in the holster tied low on his thigh with a thin, rawhide strip. All the gear was aimed at setting the female audience's hearts aflutter, but at the moment it was driving Mitch nuts. He was sunburned to a crisp.

Why he had let that socialite brat talk him into flying into Midland, then driving to Big Bend National Park for naked cliff diving, he hadn't the faintest idea. Peter was going to have a cow when he saw the pictures. The tabloid photographer must have been hanging from a tree to get the cover shot. How apt, he thought with a wry chuckle.

Oh, well, Peter would get over it. He'd rant and rave for a while, but that was all, Mitch decided. He threw in another bad hand, then shrugged when the prop technician let out a loud whoop and raked in the sizable pot.

Maybe he should call Peter and warn him, get the lecture over and done with. Mitch considered the idea while the key grip dealt a new hand. Nah . . . He wasn't in the mood to deal with one of Peter's sermons.

The arrival of a taxi pulled his attention away from the first decent hand of cards he'd had all afternoon. The cabbie got out and went around to open the door for his passenger.

"Who in their right mind would come out here in the middle of nowhere if they didn't have to?" one of the crewmen wondered as he anted up his share of the pot.

Mitch knew who it wasn't. It wasn't one of those bloodsuckers from the *International Intruder*; they were too sneaky to arrive by taxi. If he ever got his hands on one of them . . . A sick feeling hit him in the stomach. Maybe it was Peter, come to quote him chapter and verse, as he'd been doing for months over the phone.

A long, low wolf whistle from the key grip drew Mitch's gaze from a pair of aces back to the taxi— and to the woman who'd just alighted. His blue eyes collided with a mass of red curls and a dangerous abundance of curves.

She didn't look away when he gave her a blatantly frank perusal. Acting as rotten as he felt, he called out, "Hey, Red, if you're the local welcoming committee, you're late." But the pretty woman pointedly ignored him as she paid the driver and collected her baggage.

"Oh, goodie, she's staying," Mitch mumbled, tossing down one card.

The crew members smirked and hooted; Mitch knew that the macho fraternity found him quite entertaining when he chose to be—when he wasn't being a general pain in the rear.

The woman with the luscious legs, wearing a short, stretchy, peg skirt, walked toward them. "Mitch Marlow?" she inquired, stopping beside him.

He didn't bother to look up from the fresh card he'd been dealt. "That's me.... Want my autograph, do you now, darlin'?"

"Only if you sign it in blood," she answered with a pained sigh, removing her sunglasses and hanging them on her funky necklace.

"Blood...?" Mitch tried not to smirk but not very hard as he inquired, "PMS...right?"

Her pose was one of unforced confidence. His question did not alter it one iota. "Is there someplace we can go and talk—alone?" she asked.

"Hey, fellas, did you hear that? She wants to talk to me...alone."

There was laughter all around—more male bonding. "Yeah, her and twenty million other babes," the prop technician said with unmasked envy; he tossed in his cards and folded.

"Mr. Marlow..." she said, impatience lacing the formal address.

Mitch tilted back his cowboy hat with one knuckle, casually revealing his famous, sun-streaked locks. "Seems you have me at a bit of a disadvantage, you knowing my name when I don't know yours. Have we met somewhere before?"

"I'm Molly Hill," she said, offering her hand.

Mitch shook it. Not releasing it, he cocked his head at an angle and studied her, squinting into the glare of the sun.

"Molly Hill . . . Now that's a name one would remember. You an actress or something?"

She pulled her hand free, making Mitch smile. "No. I'm not an actress, and we haven't met before. I'm here representing the Ketteridge Agency. Peter Ketteridge sent me."

"Why?"

"Could we go someplace and discuss it?" she reiterated, holding her ground.

"Sure. Excuse us, will you, fellas? Come on, follow me, Red."

"It's Molly."

"Whatever," he said, taking her arm and marching her to his trailer.

"How come you aren't shooting, instead of sitting around playing poker, if the movie's over deadline?" she asked, running to keep up with him in her high heels on the uneven ground.

"We're doing an outdoor scene and we have to match the time of day with the footage we shot yesterday," Mitch answered. She had to be pretty new at her job if she didn't know that. "Have you been with Peter's agency for very long?"

"Two years," she answered when they reached the trailer. Once inside the invitingly cool trailer, he took her briefcase.

"What's in here, anyway? You've been holding it like it contains the loot from a bank job. Did Peter send you all the way out here to get me to sign some papers or something for him? Wait . . . I'll bet it's about that underwater picture, isn't it? I told him I'm not doing it, no matter how much money they're offering." He stopped and gave her a once-over. "No matter how luscious the babe he sends out here to induce me to do it."

"I'm not a lus . . . a babe," Molly said, swallowing dryly. "It's work I brought along with me, if you don't mind." She grabbed the briefcase from him. "I thought perhaps I'd be able to do it while I'm baby-sitting you."

"While you're *what?*"

"Baby-sitting you," she repeated. "That's why the agency sent me. Hasn't Mr. Ketteridge called you about it?"

"No."

"Perhaps you should call him."

"Don't worry. I intend to right now," Mitch said, moving in on her, enjoying the look on her face as the distance between them grew whisper thin. Smiling wickedly, he reached around her for the telephone.

"If you're some tabloid reporter, now would be a good time to scram," he warned, covering the mouthpiece of the phone while waiting for someone to answer.

She didn't move.

"Oh, hi. Yeah . . . is Peter in? Tell him it's Marlow. That's right, and I'm not a happy camper at the moment, so he'd best get his butt on the line, pronto."

"Get me a cold beer from the fridge, would you, Red?" Mitch said, jerking a thumb over his shoulder.

Molly carefully inched past him to the refrigerator, watching as Mitch cradled the phone against his shoulder; the modern instrument looked incongruous with his cowboy gear. She pitched him a beer from where she stood, and he caught it one-handed, just as the phone crackled back to life.

"Listen, Peter, your ah . . . practical joke . . . has arrived. Ha-ha. Real funny, Peter. I owe you one." He winked at Molly.

He opened the beer in his hand while listening to Peter; a scowl slowly replaced the look of amusement on his face.

"It's *not* a joke? Then what the hell is it?"

A little later he slammed down the receiver and stood thoughtful for a moment, then turned his attention back to her.

She didn't blink under his unswerving gaze.

"What's the verdict?" she asked finally.

"Verdict?"

She nodded. "Am I leaving or staying?"

"Oh, you're staying, all right," he answered, draining the last of his beer.

Molly cleared her throat nervously. "And it's all right with you . . . that I'm to baby-sit you until this film is wrapped?"

"I don't know." He gave her a look that was blatantly seductive. "Just how good are you at tucking in?"

Molly crossed her arms in front of her. "Forget it. I'm not your type."

"Says who?"

"Your history." She counted on her fingertips. "Blond-haired, blue-eyed, nymphet, IQ struggling to surpass two digits."

"There's a reason for that."

"One assumes."

"No, not the blond, blue-eyed, et cetera—the two-digit IQ."

"Fragile ego?" she inquired solicitously.

He shook his head. "Nope. High IQ's usually come with biting rejoinders I can live without."

"Fragile ego," she repeated, smiling smugly.

MITCH LOOKED as if he wanted to hit someone. Anger radiated off him in waves. A moment later he swung and the fight began.

"I don't think he's doing much acting, do you?" Heather Simms, the petite, blond actress who played the love interest in the film commented as she sat beside Molly in a canvas chair and tanned herself. "Whew! All that pent-up hostility makes me hot. What Mitch Marlow needs is a real woman to relieve the pain he's in. If you ask me he's past ready to feel alive again."

The lust in the rising star's voice spelled trouble to Molly. Heather was married to an insanely jealous superstar wrestler. Sonny and Heather Simms's legendary marital spats during their three-year marriage had snagged even more tabloid covers than Mitch. Molly knew Heather's wandering eye could spell disaster.

"I thought you were married to Sonny Simms," Molly reminded her.

"I'm married, but I'm not dead," Heather said, while they both enjoyed the view of Mitch dusting off the seat of his outlaw's britches after the fight scene. He adjusted the low-slung gun belt on his hip, causing Heather to sigh. "And some temptations are just too hard to resist, you know."

The character actor playing opposite Mitch was rigged out in cowboy gear, too, only it didn't look dangerously sexy on him, merely serviceable. The character actor was beefier and taller, with the right menacing look, but Mitch's grace when he moved took away the other actor's advantage of height and weight. Mitch was pure poetry in motion, with a natural athlete's perfect coordination.

There was nothing pure about the thoughts Mitch interrupted, however, when he turned to Molly and called, "Hey, Red, mind getting me another pair of leather gloves? I just busted this pair."

Stripping off the gloves, he tossed them to her. It took great deal of effort on her part to resist the temptation to bring them to her nose.

Setting aside the paperwork she'd been pretending to do, she realized she'd been right about his appeal in the flesh. While his talent awed her, his charisma made her want to follow in his wake. He was intense and full of life; hiding his pain most of the time by playing pranks, catching his fellow actors off guard. It took every ounce of self-control she owned not to stammer, gawk or faint in his presence. She was in over her head without a lifeline in sight. How could one man's sheer, physical beauty make her so addle-brained? She had to get a grip on her feelings before she made a fool of herself and lost this opportunity. She had to remember this was the fantasy world of moviemaking.

Rising to carry out Mitch's request, she realized she'd been waiting for an excuse to take a closer look at his trailer. Last night she'd merely glimpsed it before he'd introduced her around and taken her baggage to the trailer she shared with the "best boy," who was, in this instance, a woman. Her name was Angie, and her job was to assist the key grip with setting up the physical operations of the film, making sure everything that was supposed to happen did so.

Inside the trailer, Molly gave her curiosity a few minutes' free rein before beginning a search for the gloves.

While she didn't actually snoop into the closets or closed drawers, she did take a visual inventory of what lay in the open. A pair of expensive sunglasses that he never seemed to wear, a worn deck of poker cards, a pair of Day-Glo shorts wadded next to a stack of paperback Westerns, a skateboard... A skateboard? And...uh...a shiny packet of foil-wrapped condoms.

She stared at them; perhaps he wasn't suicidal, after all.

"Take anything you need, darlin'," Mitch said, startling her as he came up behind her, close enough for her to feel the whisper of his warm breath on her neck. She'd been so lost in her examination that she hadn't heard him enter the trailer at all.

"I...I was looking...ah...for your gloves," she said, sure her face was beet red.

"You're in the wrong trailer."

"What?"

"Extras are in the costume trailer," he explained. "I realized you didn't know that, after I saw you begin heading this way."

"Oh."

He nodded to the shiny foil packet, then reached around her. Opening a drawer, he tossed in the packet of condoms to join several dozen others. Grinning like a wicked highwayman about to take a lady's virtue, he said, "It gets pretty boring making movies, with all the waiting around between scenes. One has to find ways of entertaining oneself."

"Is your trailer the equivalent of the costume trailer when it comes to safe sex for the whole crew, or is your ego that outsize?"

He laughed, a rich, seductive laugh that crawled up her spine, trailing sweet suggestion. "Water balloons. I use them for water balloon fights, you goose." There was a cool stare on his face when she turned and he added, "Mostly."

"Oh." Molly was furious to find herself continually tongue-tied in his presence. Normally a glib comeback tripped off her tongue, but then, normally she didn't find herself mere inches from the country's leading heartthrob, who also just happened to star in her own private fantasies.

"Listen, since you're here and everything, would you mind doing me one more favor?" Mitch asked, pulling off his leather vest and beginning to unbutton his dusty chambray shirt.

"I . . . ah . . ."

When he pulled the shirt from his pants and shrugged completely free of it, she closed her eyes and stood rooted to the spot, feeling for all the world like some nineteenth-century spinster.

She took a quick breath of surprise when she felt him reach around her again for something in the drawer, but her eyes flew wide open at his next words. "Here, this lubricant might help."

Molly looked down, to see his long, slender fingers wrapped around a bottle of green herbal lotion. "My back," he indicated, turning it to her, "feels like something out of a packet of Crispy Critters. Would you mind rubbing some of this on it for me?"

"Oh . . . okay," she stammered, taking the bottle from him.

"I'll just sit down on the edge of the bed, so it will be easier for you to reach," he offered. The bed groaned under his weight, echoing her own discomfort at being confronted by the wide expanse of naked, sinewy flesh.

Yeah, sitting down was good, she thought, fearing she might go completely weak-kneed, once she began touching his bare skin.

Opening the bottle, she squeezed some of the globby contents onto her palm and tentatively raised her hand to his bare back. Taking a deep breath, she touched his feverish skin, her fingers trembling slightly.

"Ahh . . ." Mitch sighed as she began massaging the green goo into his back until it turned clear and disappeared.

"It smells like lime Jell-O," she noted, letting her hands follow the contours of his back; it had a very masculine, triangular shape.

"Feel free to lick anytime."

She didn't reply, but continued to stroke the ointment onto his back, just for the feel of his skin beneath her touch. It was impossible to touch, to press skin to skin and remain remote, as she'd promised herself she would. Finally realizing what she was doing, she stopped.

"All done?" he asked, glancing over his shoulder.

"Yes." *All done in* was more like it, she thought, putting the lid back on the bottle.

"Let me give you some advice, Red. Never go cliff diving naked, without protection." He lowered his voice to a whisper. "You get burned *everywhere.*"

"Including the press," Molly commented dryly.

"Touché," Mitch said, tossing the lotion back into the still open drawer. "I guess ol' Peter was plenty steamed when he saw the pictures that landed me on the cover of the supermarket tabloid, huh?"

"Like a lobster."

"Oh, well, at least there was some benefit to it, as things turned out."

"There was?"

"Sure. I got me a baby-sitter. Gosh, I haven't had one of those since I was—oh, say eleven or so. Her name was Monica and she taught me how to—"

"I don't think I want to know," Molly said, rolling her eyes heavenward.

He told her, anyway. "Skateboard." He nodded to the one leaning in the corner of the trailer. "What did you think she taught me, goose?"

She didn't answer, aware that her silence incriminated her.

"Now, I'm assuming you're a tad older than Monica was at sixteen, so does that mean you're going to teach me more advanced things than skateboarding?" he asked coolly.

"That's right," she answered, deflecting the direction his conversation was taking. "I'm here to teach you how to stay alive."

3

By late Saturday afternoon Molly was feeling pretty good about the way things were going. Mitch maintained his posture of cool indifference toward her being on the set as his baby-sitter. For almost a full week nothing untoward had happened. Maybe, just maybe, the gods would continue to smile on her, and this gig would come off uneventfully.

It could happen. Mitch could also be setting her up, lulling her into a false sense of security.

Having managed to get most of the paperwork she'd brought with her cleared up, she'd borrowed one of the paperback Westerns from Mitch's trailer. It wasn't doing a very good job of holding her attention, but then, it was up against some pretty tough competition—the face of the nineties. He was in the process of doing take number twenty, one of the difficult, climactic fight scenes, and she'd watched his frustration grow with every take.

How long, she wondered, before Mitch Marlow lost his legendary cool in front of the camera?

She wasn't to find out.

He got take twenty-one down dead solid, and it was a print. His pleasure was self-evident, judging by the war whoop he let out when he picked himself up from the dirt, giving the tired crew a mock bow.

His eyes finally rested on Molly. Staying in character, he ambled over to where she sat, knocking the dust from his leather chaps with his cowboy hat. Reaching her side, he closed the book and said, "Playtime."

"You mean bedtime, don't you?" she asked, retrieving the book from him. He looked exhausted; the shoot had begun at dawn.

"Why, Red, I didn't know you cared," Mitch said, lifting an eyebrow.

"Don't flatter yourself."

Rather than appearing affronted, her words seemed to amuse him. "Ah, ah . . . Remember, it's in your job description that you have to tuck me in," he dared her, leaning close.

"Wrong. My job is to keep you out of trouble. Period."

"Then I guess you're right, after all," he said with a shrug. "Tucking me in wouldn't be such a good idea."

Pulling up a chair, he sat down beside her. "You got any plans for what's left of the weekend? Got a boyfriend flying in?"

"No boyfriend."

"Really?"

"Really. How about you?"

"Despite my regular appearances in the tabloids, I can assure you I don't have a boyfriend."

"You know what I mean. Am I going to have to deal with Miss Debutante flying in and trying to coax you into another crazy stunt?"

"No. I don't think her daddy, the banker, was any too pleased with the press last weekend generated—which was exactly the whole point of her doing it. You can rest assured, I won't be doing any naked cliff diving this weekend."

"Peter will be thrilled to hear it."

"What? Do you write daily reports on my behavior for Peter?" he demanded, fixing her with a cold stare.

"We keep in touch. We wouldn't have to if you'd deal with your brother's death," she said heatedly. There, now it was out in the open. She wondered how Mitch would deal with her blunt words. No matter. He had to deal with the reality of his brother's death, and the sooner, the better.

That she knew firsthand. She'd allowed her grief and guilt over her older brother's accidental drowning to steal her childhood. Joey had wanted to be an astronomer, so she'd let her parents talk her into becoming one. She'd let her parents talk her into everything.

For some crazy reason she'd thought if she was a good enough girl, maybe Joey wouldn't be dead, after all. And Mitch believed that if he was bad enough, Matthew wouldn't be dead, either.

The silence continued to stretch out between them, disturbed only by the sounds of the crew finishing up for the day. Finally Mitch spoke, breaking down the wall that had suddenly sprung up between them. *"I miss Matthew, damn it."*

"I'm really sorry. I know how you feel," Molly said, hearing the pain in his voice.

"No, you *don't* know how I feel," Mitch retorted angrily. "Everyone keeps telling me they know how I feel with so damn much compassion. Well, I don't want their compassion. And I sure as hell don't deserve it. If it wasn't for me, he'd still be alive. Every night when I close my eyes I see the horrifying crash, the debris flying everywhere, and Matt's car turning over and over."

"You're not responsible for Matthew's death. It was an accident," Molly reasoned, touching his arm. "Surely you can't blame yourself for something that—"

"Matthew flew over for the premiere of *Dangerous*.

"It was the night before the race. He knew better. He should have been at home, getting his rest, not out partying the night away with me. The flight back and the residual jet lag are what killed him."

Mitch stared into space. "His reflexes would have been sharper, but for his coming to celebrate my movie."

"He wouldn't want—"

"He'd want to be alive." Mitch cut her off, throwing himself out of his chair and stalking away. His slumping shoulders evidenced the black mood that had settled over him like a villain's cloak.

Molly watched him go, touched by the anger, the guilt in his declaration—a declaration she knew he'd not meant to make. Anger and guilt had loosened his tongue, but his admission hadn't freed him. She knew that until he found some measure of solace, he would be looking for any escape from his grief, not much caring what form it took.

BACK IN HIS TRAILER, Mitch picked up the phone and dialed the Ketteridge Agency.

"Listen, Peter . . ." he began, caught off guard at first when Peter answered his own phone. "Ah . . . this . . . ah, this isn't working out."

"What's wrong? Is there a problem with the movie? Don't tell me this. I don't want to hear it, Marlow. What have you gone and messed up now?"

"Nothing. There's no problem with the movie. The movie is on schedule, maybe even a little ahead of schedule."

"Then it's working."

"Not for me. I want you to call off your baby-sitter, you hear?"

"No can do, Mitch. The studio brass insist."

Mitch swore beneath his breath and wondered whether to believe his wily friend.

"You ought to be ashamed of yourself for belly-aching. If your behavior weren't so out of control, you wouldn't need to be sat on," Peter said.

"Yeah, well, Ms. Molly is real big on control. You got to get rid of her, Peter, she's driving me nuts."

"Nuts?"

"Yeah, nuts. She watches me like a hawk. You'd think I was some actor always in his cups she was trying to keep sober. Hell, I can hardly take a pee without her tagging along."

"What'd she do? Make some disparaging remark and bruise your ego?" Peter asked.

Mitch ignored the feeble attempt at sarcasm. "I don't need a baby-sitter."

"That's not what the tabloid headlines showed."

"Okay, I don't *want* a keeper."

"Why not?"

Mitch refused to go into that. He wouldn't admit to himself, much less to Peter, that somehow Molly was getting to him.... She might make him care—about this movie, his career, maybe even about her. She'd already made him voice his fears about Matthew's death, when he hadn't even whispered them to himself.

"Look, I'm not planning on offing myself, if that's what you're afraid of. You'll get your fifteen percent. If I have to have a baby-sitter, replace her with someone else."

"You mean someone you can charm the pants off."

"Peter, you have way too active an imagination."

"I don't need an imagination, when the *International Intruder* has pictures."

"Screw the *International Intruder*."

"She's staying. Get used to it," Peter said and hung up.

Mitch grumbled beneath his breath and went to take his shower. He didn't want to get used to Molly Hill.

Something warned him that wouldn't be a very good idea at all.

The good idea was to bed her.

Take her to bed and off his mind.

Once he buried himself in her soft curves, he wouldn't be wanting her comfort. Wouldn't care what she thought about what he did. Wouldn't care what she thought about him.

HOURS LATER, Molly returned to the trailer she shared with Angie, tired of watching the regular evening poker game. The key grip had gone off in search of some local talent, so Angie had been invited to take his place. After showing initial reluctance, she'd allowed them to coax her into playing, only to make them wish they hadn't.

The youngest sister in a family of boys, she'd told Molly, Angie had mastered the game in her somewhat misspent youth, so it had been hard for Molly to contain her amusement as she watched Angie fleece the guys; even the intense, young director had lost some heavy coin.

Mitch had tried to talk Angie into sitting on his lap to bring him luck. Angie had rebuffed him, saying he needed a new line. Heather had then plopped into Mitch's lap, uninvited.

Molly had fumed and tried to read the movie script, listening for Mitch's voice over the snippets of conversation that drifted toward the trailer.

His sexy good looks turned her on, but it was his voice that blew her away. Its rich timbre sent her blood coursing, her pulse racing and her imagination into erotic overdrive.

Unfortunately, he apparently had the same effect on Heather Simms—Heather, who had the confidence in her own body's appeal that Molly did not. Heather, who was every man's type. Heather, who could juggle a husband, a lover and still have time for lunch.

Being born a blonde and petite in a culture that worshiped both was Heather's good fortune. But throwing herself at Mitch was pure opportunism.

Being only human, Molly couldn't help envying Heather's upcoming love scene with Mitch. The very thought of it brought on a frisson of jealousy.

The voices outside grew distant, her eyelids fluttered, and she began to imagine herself in Heather's role....

Looking down, she found herself dressed in red velvet, sitting before a mirrored dressing table.

Red? Red wasn't her color. Her dressmaker had made a terrible mistake. She tugged on the bodice cut far too low that pressed her breasts together, showing amazing cleavage.

She was going to have to speak to . . . Funny, she couldn't remember her dressmaker's name. Wait! No, it was Angie. Yes, that was it.

She'd have to wear the dress tonight, of course; it was a present from her father for her birthday. But in the morning she'd talk with Angie. If she'd only kept her mind off her card playing and on her sewing, this wouldn't have happened. Card playing? Now where had she gotten the idea her seamstress played poker? Women didn't gamble, only men— even if it was 1880.

Suddenly the door behind her opened.

Her eyes widened when she saw the outlaw's reflection—Mitch's reflection—in her dressing-table mirror. Shaggy, blond hair fell to his broad shoulders. Trail dust clung to him—he was either in a hurry to get somewhere or away from someone.

She opened her mouth to scream, but closed it when he drew his pearl-handled revolver from the holster that rode low on his hip and leveled it at her.

"You're an . . ." She swallowed dryly, sinking to the delicate brocade-covered bench.

"That's right, I'm an outlaw. And that was a real smart move, your not screaming, miss," Mitch said, studying her in the mirror with his deep blue eyes. Raising his eyes to meet hers once again, he pushed up the brim of his black Stetson with the tip of his gun barrel, then holstered it.

"My, my, but you're a sight for sore eyes," he said, coming up behind her. "'Course, I've been looking at nothing but a trail of posse dust for the last couple of hours."

"What . . . why are you . . . what do you want?" she asked, forcing the words through chattering teeth.

His blue eyes raked her again, this time accompanied by a lazy, wicked smile. Leaving her, his eyes surveyed her bedchamber and came to rest on the copper tub of cooling bathwater in the alcove to the left. "I think a bath for starters . . ." he said, drawing her to her feet to face him, his forefinger tilting her chin, so that she was forced to look at him. "Then we can discuss what other favors you might bestow on me."

She pulled herself free, hitting the bench of her dressing table with the backs of her knees. "I think you should leave," she said imperiously, keeping her chin high.

He chuckled. "Surely, miss, your daddy has warned you about defying the wishes of an outlaw," he said, ambling over to the tub and removing his soft leather gloves, trailing his fingertips through the few remaining bubbles. Raising his fingertips to his nose, he sniffed. His eyebrows rose. "The water still carries your scent."

She felt herself blush to the shade of her red velvet gown and sat tongue-tied by his provocative action.

Taking off his hat, he threw it onto the bedpost. Its masculine presence was a marked contrast to the frills of the bed linens. He was so out of place in this soft, feminine room. So why was her heart racing? She turned to the outlaw, who, she saw to her horror, was undoing the kerchief at his throat.

"But you can't!" she exclaimed. He shrugged out of his leather vest and began unbuttoning his shirt.

"Stop it and leave this very minute, before my father comes upstairs and finds you here in my bedroom!" Her words were a feeble protest—she was way too fascinated by what Mitch was uncovering to scream.

Mitch chuckled again. "Right now your father can't find his cuff links. I heard him swearing about it as I sneaked up the back stairs.

"Don't even think about screaming," he added, drawing his pistol from its holster, only to lay it on the windowsill beside the copper tub. "You see, if your daddy should come up here, I'd have to shoot him—and you wouldn't want that, now, would you?"

She watched, dry-mouthed, as he untied and unbuckled his holster, hanging it over her dressing screen. His hands went to the waistband of his britches.

"But you can't...."

"Watch me ... or turn around if you don't have the courage—or womanly curiosity—in which case I'll be sorely disappointed. I do so hate women without spirit."

"And I hate you," she flared, turning her back to him, aware that her eyes were brimming with tears of frustration.

"Not yet, you don't...."

She heard the jangle of his spurs as his boots dropped to the floor, followed by the whoosh of his chaps and pants. Splashing sounds accompanied him when he stepped into the copper tub.

"You can turn around now," he said.

"No, thank you," she answered, letting her voice drip polite sarcasm.

"Suit yourself."

She heard the sound of a bar of soap plopping into the water, then he began to hum.

Humming! She wondered if she was quick enough to reach his gun.

"Ah, miss, I've thought of another favor you can do for me."

She spun around, incensed at the man's gall. Mitch removed the small cigar he held clenched between his straight white teeth and motioned with it to the candle burning beside the bed. "I need a light."

She glared at him.

"Now," he said impatiently.

She went to her bedside table and brought the candle to him, shaking with fury.

He clenched the small cigar between his teeth once again and leaned forward for her to light it.

Too late, he saw a smile flit across her lips; she slowly dropped the candle into the tub of water, making a splash big enough to ruin his cigar.

"That wasn't too smart, miss," he growled.

"I thought you liked your women to have spirit," she said, taking care to stay out of his reach.

"You could have ruined me. . . ."

"That was the general idea."

"You are an innocent, aren't you?"

"No."

"Then take off your gown."

"What?"

"You heard me. I said, take off your gown. I want you to scrub my back, and if you don't want to completely ruin that pretty velvet, you'd best take it off."

"I'm not taking off anything."

"Do I have to get out of this tub and make you, miss?" he threatened.

"No! No. Okay, I'll do it, but you have to promise to keep your head turned away."

He laughed. "I promise."

She looked at him doubtfully, then bent to retrieve his kerchief, advancing toward him.

"What do you think you're doing?" he demanded.

"Blindfolding you," she answered, proceeding to do just that.

"You're taking all the fun out of this," he complained.

"Not for me."

After allowing her to blindfold him, he listened to the sensuous sounds of her removing her dress and smiled.

"Hand me the soap," she said, moving to the tub in just her petticoats.

Locating it, he held it just beyond her reach, his smile turning into a grin.

When she reached for the bar, he grabbed her hand, catching her off balance. She fell into the tub with a splash.

"What do you think you're doing?" she sputtered. The water was seeping through her petticoats, making them completely transparent.

"Exactly what you want me to, Red," he whispered, closing his hand over her breast; his lips met hers.

"Molly! Wake up, Molly!"

"What...?" Molly asked, blinking the sleep from her eyes to find Angie standing over her in an agitated state.

"It's Mitch. I thought you'd want to know."

"Mitch? What ... what's happened?" The sensual dream was still clouding her mind.

"He's just driven off with some of the crew and a few of the locals."

"He's left? Why? Where were they going?"

"To a place called the Flats."

"The Flats?"

Angie nodded. "They're going to race. One of the locals challenged Mitch." The agitation in her voice was clear. "Because of Heather. She was flirting with all the men. One of the locals got jealous. Unfortunately he made some crack about Mitch's hotshot racing brother, Matthew."

"Oh, no!"

Molly closed her eyes. Taking a deep breath to calm herself, she waited a moment, then opened her eyes again. "Angie, can you take me to this place . . . the Flats?"

"Yeah, I think I can find it from what they were talking about. It didn't sound to be too far away from here."

Seconds later they were heading out. Angie wasn't following the local speed limit as she swung the car around a curve, fishtailing it.

"Be careful!" Molly yelled over the roar of the engine.

"I don't think there's time to be careful," Angie said. "In the Midwest they call the kind of race Mitch has gotten himself into playing chicken—you know, as in James Dean's *Rebel Without a Cause*."

"Oh, my God—step on it!"

4

MOLLY WATCHED the rolling hills of the Meramec Valley speed past in a dark blur, her mind busy with images of impending disaster. She'd been foolish to believe Mitch's promise that he wouldn't try anything dangerous. He'd only told her what she wanted to hear, as he'd no doubt been doing with women since his very first back-seat romance.

She tried to remember how the movie *Rebel Without a Cause* had ended. All she could recall was how James Dean had ended up in real life— dead in the wreckage of his speeding car.

The atmosphere inside their car was thick with worry. Neither she nor Angie spoke about their fears while they continually scanned the roadsides for some sign of the racers or the Flats.

There was no sign of either.

It was Molly who finally gave voice to her fears. "Oh, Angie, what if we don't find them in time? What if we can't find the Flats?"

"We'll find them," Angie vowed. "Remember those six older brothers I told you I had? Well, they were always trying to elude their pesky younger sister when I was growing up, but I always managed to track them down."

A few miles farther down the highway Angie slammed on the brakes and brought the car to an abrupt halt, tires squealing. She motioned to Molly. "Look over there."

"Where?" A clump of trees obscured Molly's view.

Angie pulled the car off the highway, onto a dirt road, and headed for a clearing, where a small group of cars and people were gathered.

She had barely brought the car to a stop again, when Molly flung open her car door and began running toward two cars sitting side by side with their engines racing. A kid with a white handkerchief stood nearby. He raised his arm and yelled, "Ready, set, go!"

The kid dropped the white handkerchief and both cars raced past her. Molly's desperate, "Stop!" was drowned by the roaring engines.

Molly watched in dismay as the cars careened toward the cliff. Her heart pounded when Mitch began inching ahead.

"Why doesn't someone stop them?" she demanded, looking accusingly at the crowd. Mitch was just like her brother, who'd shown off by swimming bank to bank in a river with dangerous currents. Tears formed in her eyes. She couldn't watch someone die stupidly again.

She couldn't.

"Don't worry, Molly. I've seen Mitch race with his brother Matthew before for fun. He has tremendous, innate skill, just as Matthew did. He'll be all right," Angie reassured her, clutching her by the arm.

Molly shook her head, not believing Angie's hopeful words for a moment.

There was no way this could come to a good end. As she watched the driver in the souped-up model with a red paint job and a design of yellow flames across its hood edge closer to Mitch's car, she had to fight not to close her eyes. Both cars continued their game of cat and mouse. Their driving was reckless, and the distance between the cars could be measured in inches. The two drivers appeared to be calling out taunts to each other as they raced ever closer to the cliff's edge.

"Where does the race end?" Molly asked, glaring at Heather, who looked excited. At least the key grip from the movie company looked a little on the white side of pale.

"It will end one way or another in a few minutes," one of the locals informed her, his manner one of bored nonchalance.

"What—what does he mean, one way or the other?" Molly stammered, looking at Angie.

The local's grin was obscene. "Either one of them turns chicken and stops or . . ."

"Or . . . ?" Molly stared at him, eyes wide, hearing her voice sink to a whisper.

The local shrugged. "There's bluffs at the end of the Flats, an' after that the Meramec River. And after that, well, it don't matter none."

"You've got to stop them!" she pleaded. "This is insane!"

"Too late," the local man said, shaking his head. "You can't stop them now."

"I can try."

Before anyone could move, Molly grabbed the keys from Angie's hand and headed for their car at a dead run.

"No!" Angie cried, but Molly paid no heed.

Molly didn't know what she was going to do, but she had to try to stop the race. Flooring the gas pedal, she began traveling across the flats toward the racers.

Now she had a better view of the two cars, both of which were quickly running out of ground. She prayed silently and breathed a sigh of blessed relief when one of the cars turned to one side, quitting the race at the last second.

It was the challenger—not Mitch—who'd come to his senses and quit.

Molly decreased her speed. It was going to be okay. Now Mitch could stop, too. He'd proven he wasn't chicken and he'd upheld his twin brother's reputation.

But he didn't stop.

Molly saw the car become airborne. A scream froze in her throat as the car sailed off the cliff, seeming to hang in the air for a moment before it began to drop, flipping end over end until it was out of sight.

"Oh God, no!" she exclaimed, stopping her car and getting out to race to the edge of the bluff.

"It's not my fault," the other driver shouted as she passed him. "He's crazy!"

In the distance Molly could hear the sound of engines; the crowd must be coming to see what had happened.

Trembling, she reached the edge of the bluff, not wanting to see what she knew lay below. She wiped at the tears and looked down at the flaming wreck. Mitch had finally succeeded in joining his brother.

"Hey Red, why are you crying? I won."

Molly squinted against the smoke rising from the burning wreckage. She choked back tears and wrinkled her nose at the acrid smell fouling the air. Hope flickered as she searched the steep embankment of the dark bluff for a sign of life.

Had she really heard Mitch's voice? Or was she only hallucinating, unwilling to accept the fact that she had failed?

"Hey, Red, over here!"

A brief scurry of pebbles slid down the bluff and she followed the sound.

"Mitch!" she cried, sighting the small outcropping, where he'd gained a tenuous hold on a branch of scrub pine.

He was alive!

He was scratched up, covered in dust from head to toe, and his handsome face was streaked with dirt, but he was alive.

And she was going to kill him. "You—you selfish bastard. What were you thinking? Didn't you realize you could have been killed?"

"No loss, Red. No loss."

The bleakness of his voice overpowered her anger. He was only trying to escape . . . outrun . . . outrace the pain and guilt he felt over his brother's death.

"Are you badly hurt?" she asked, sympathy replacing her initial fury.

He shot her a lopsided grin and winced as he tried to gain a more secure toehold. "I'm a bit banged up, as you may have noticed. And I imagine I'll be sore as hell come tomorrow. But all that's small potatoes. What really hurts badly is your harsh opinion of me, Red."

"I told you to quit calling me that."

"Deal. You quit calling me Jerkface, and I won't call you Red. So, now that we have that out of the way, do you think you might give me a hand here? I'm beginning to lose my grip, and though I'm truly enjoying our little chat, I don't much care for the idea of becoming a packet of Crispy Critters if I fall into that mess below."

Tires squealed and car doors slammed; the others came running to see the wreck. Finding Mitch alive, they eagerly pulled him to safety.

Once he was on his feet again, Heather rushed to his side, all jiggle and giggle in her tight jeans and T-shirt. Jumping up and down, she hugged him, exclaiming, "You won, Mitch! You won! You're so . . . so . . ."

"I believe dumb is the word," Molly grumbled. Walking toward Angie, she moaned, "How am I ever going to keep *this* stunt out of the tabloids, with all these witnesses?"

Angie shook her head. "There must be some way, but I admit I don't have a clue what it is."

Molly glanced at the small crowd. The local she'd been talking to earlier walked over.

"You with him?" he asked, indicating Mitch.

"Him?" Molly asked, puzzled. With all the fuss Heather was making over Mitch, how could this man believe Molly was involved with him?

The bearded man nodded. "Yeah. You with the movie company that's filmin' that Western at the caverns about Jesse James?"

Molly nodded, finally understanding. "Yes, yes, I am. I'm his agent, sort of."

"Then you're who I want to talk to."

"Me—why?"

"You know that old gray car Mitch Marlow was driving, the one that's a goner? Well, I loaned it to him. It belonged to me."

"And you want to be compensated for it. How much were you wanting? If we can settle on a reasonable sum, I'll get you a check drawn up."

"It's not money I'm after."

"You want us to replace the car? I don't know. It looked pretty, ah . . ."

"Yeah, it was pretty beat up. You don't think I'd lend out my best car, do you?" A crafty look settled on his face; he must be getting to what he really wants, Molly thought. "I was thinking I wouldn't mind being in that picture you're making."

That was it. The answer to her dilemma. Molly wouldn't have to lose her job, after all.

"I'll talk to the director. I'm sure we can arrange a small, walk-on part for you," she assured the man, ignoring the fact that she had no authority whatsoever to do so.

Acting on impulse, she called for the crowd's attention. "How would you all like to be extras in the movie Mitch Marlow is making?" Molly asked, waiting anxiously for their response.

It wasn't long in coming. Their looks of surprise were quickly followed by cheers of agreement. She only hoped she could convince the director it was a great idea.

"Okay, then it's agreed. But here's the deal. We'll hire the lot of you as extras for one day of filming on *Jesse*, but if any of you talk to the press about this little incident, we have this thing called a cutting-room floor. If any one of you talks, the lot of you will be edited out, understand?"

The crowd nodded in tacit agreement.

"Okay, then," Molly said. "I'd like to thank you all for your cooperation. Angie here will take down your names and give you the details when everything is set up."

As the small group crowded around Angie, who'd hastily pulled a notebook and pen from her purse, Mitch joined Molly.

"That's some promise you made," he said, studying her. "You really think you can pull it off? Temperamental directors have this thing about being in control."

"I wouldn't have made the promise if I didn't plan on keeping it," Molly answered pointedly, directing her anger toward him. "You could have been killed tonight, and so could the other driver. At the very least, this could have ended up in the news, effectively putting the finishing touch on both our careers. I thought we had an agreement."

"I didn't go looking for trouble, it found me," Mitch countered, apparently shrugging off responsibility.

Molly just looked at him, not buying his excuse. "Do me a favor, will you?"

"Sure, what?"

"Quit pretending not to care. Stop denying you're in pain. Just stop—stop pretending."

Mitch stood there for a moment, looking pale and solemn. His voice was no more than a whisper when he said, "Pretending is what I do. It's the only thing I'm good at . . . it's who I am."

THE FOLLOWING AFTERNOON Molly was in the costume trailer with Angie. Angie was gamely filling in for the wardrobe mistress, who'd had to leave the set due to an illness in her family. Now her dark eyes were intent on the seam of the period gown she was taking in to fit Heather.

"Mitch's been pretty quiet today," Angie said, finishing off the seam. "Do you think nearly killing his fool self last night had some effect on him? Or could it be he's plotting his next harebrained escapade for the cover of the *International Intruder?*"

"I'm surprised those bloodsuckers weren't around to capture last night's fiasco on film," Molly said pensively. "Perhaps Mitch is withdrawn because he's readying himself for a scene. I've noticed he always gets quiet before shooting. I think it's some sort of mental preparation, a kind of ritual he goes through. When he's finally ready to do the scene, you can actually notice the transformation—he literally becomes the character he's playing. It's eerie. Then once he relaxes into the part he's playing, all the action takes place in his eyes."

"Yeah, those eyes. Couldn't you just drown in them?" The look on Angie's face was positively sinful.

"Angie?"

Angie laughed, a sexy, bawdy laugh that bounced off the walls of the trailer. "Well, Mitch is one great looker. It's lucky for you my taste runs to the more cerebral type. There's something about a man in a pair of glasses that makes me want to fog them up, you know? But don't worry, Molly, your secret is safe with me."

"My secret?" Molly asked, handing Angie the pair of scissors she'd motioned for.

"You know," Angie said, looking up and grinning at her after she'd snipped a thread, "you don't have to be coy with me. I'm not going to spill the beans about you being warm for Mitch Marlow's form."

Molly felt herself blushing even as she uttered her denial. "I'm sure I don't know what you're talking about. I haven't said anything that would lead you to believe I have even the slightest interest in Mitch Marlow. For me, this is a job. Nothing more."

"A job?" Angie hooted. "You're trying to tell me baby-sitting Hollywood's hottest heartthrob is nothing more than a job to you? I suppose you haven't noticed his cowboy swagger, or that when he smiles, infrequent though that may be, you don't feel like crossing your legs . . . real tight. You'd better have your pulse checked to make sure you're alive, if Mitch Marlow doesn't stir up feelings of lust when he—"

"Well, lust, sure," Molly admitted. "But it's just chemistry, Angie. I would never allow myself to become involved with a movie star. I'm not the one who's suicidal, remember?"

"I don't understand. Most women would leap at the opportunity to be Mitch Marlow's main squeeze."

Molly just looked at Angie. "Think about it. He's starred in my fantasies since his first movie—mine and every other woman's. And he knows it. He's not going to settle for just one woman, and I couldn't bear being just one more in a long list of women whose hearts he's broken."

"Aren't you being a little cynical?" Angie said.

"Am I? It isn't necessary to use more than one hand to count on your fingers the number of happy Hollywood marriages."

Angie nodded. "I have to admit you're right about that." Finishing Heather's dress, she shook out the wrinkles and held it up to see the result of her handiwork.

Gazing at the size two gown, Molly sighed.

"What?" Angie asked, hanging it up with Heather's other costumes.

"I don't know. Sometimes I feel intimidated by a world that has just one measure of female perfection. Can you believe that decades of women have been brainwashed into insecurity by a seemingly innocent toy they were given to play with as children?"

"What are you talking about?"

"Barbie. Because of her we all believe subconsciously that the perfect female is a blonde with diamond-shaped spaces between her legs at ankle, knee and thigh top. Space between the ears is undoubtedly an added bonus. Why is beauty equated with having legs that go all the way to one's armpits?"

"You aren't serious. You can't really believe that junk, Molly."

"Not intellectually, maybe. But it is emotional baggage. All it takes some days is one Heather Simms to make me feel as if I'm a float in the Rose Bowl Parade. Having these wild, orange curls doesn't help. It's like having a neon sign on your head."

"You're being dumb."

"I know. I know. I've accepted the fact that I will never be a Barbie doll and I like who I am now.

Well, I could deal with losing ten pounds permanently, instead of every bathing-suit season. Haven't you ever felt you didn't measure up?"

"Are you kidding? I had even more impossible standards to measure up to than Barbie. I had six brothers, remember. G.I. Joe was my role model. Mostly I was judged by how well I could shoot a basket or slide into second base."

"When I was growing up, I was never allowed to sweat. My parents were overprotective and encouraged me to do quiet, safe activities." Molly smiled ruefully. "Speaking of G.I. Joe, though, it's funny, but in a way he has become the new role model for female perfection in the nineties."

"G.I. Joe?" Angie looked at Molly as if she'd taken leave of her senses.

"Well, take a look at Linda Hamilton in *Terminator II*. Heck, she even makes G.I. Joe look like a wimp."

"Yeah, she had a certain appeal, but can you imagine how much time she had to spend in a gym to look like that? Not only could you not have a life, but it must be painful."

"I think the sinewy muscles Linda Hamilton displayed in that movie appealed more to the female audience than to men, and they appealed to women because they were a show of female empowerment. But since I don't like to sweat, I'll have to be empowered by my mind. Besides, I agree with a writer friend of mine who says, 'No pain...no pain.'"

At that moment the key grip knocked on the door and yelled, "Call for you Ms. Hill. It's a Mr. Ketteridge from L.A."

"Speaking of pain..." Molly grumbled and headed out to take the call. It could only mean trouble.

"Hello, Mr. Ketteridge."

"How are things going?"

"Everything is fine. No problems so far."

"And Mitch?"

"He's been a perfect angel."

"Mitch has never been any kind of angel."

Molly ran a hand through her curls and said in her sweetest voice, "You haven't seen him on the front pages of the *International Intruder*, have you?"

Ketteridge didn't answer, but asked instead about the locals the director had complained about hiring. "Why did you hire them?"

"No special reason, Mr. Ketteridge. I just thought it would be good public relations. If something did happen, it would help keep a lid on things to have the goodwill of the locals."

"I hope you know what you're doing. You certainly don't know anything about picking mechanics."

"I tried. I can't help it if you didn't like the mechanic I found for your temperamental sports car, Mr. Ketteridge." Molly sighed. All of the agency trainees performed personal errands for the owner.

"I could have put a kid through college with the money I've spent on maintaining that car... two kids."

Molly rolled her eyes at Angie as she pulled up a director's chair alongside, and went on listening to Peter sputter away, holding the phone a foot from her ear. Putting it back to her ear, she tried calming him down. "Listen, why don't you call your mother? She always has advice for you. Maybe she knows the name of a good mechanic. One you'd like better than the one I found for you in the Yellow Pages."

"I'm not calling my mother. She drives me nuts!"

"But she loves you. She's lonely since your father died. That's why she calls you all the time."

"All she talks about is when am I going to get married and give her grandchildren."

"Maybe you need to think of something to distract her."

"Like what?"

"I don't know what." She looked at Angie and shook her head, while Angie grinned her understanding; how helpless men could be sometimes! "Wait, I think I've got an idea," Molly said into the phone. "Why don't you have your mother test all the recipes in that cookbook the rock singer's wife is writing?"

"Really, Ms. Hill. The publisher has a professional doing that."

"But your mother doesn't know it. It will make her feel useful, and she'll adore the idea that she's helping out her only son."

Molly held the phone away from her ear once again, while her boss ran through a litany of complaints about his mother's intrusion in his life. Returning the phone to her ear, she tried again to calm him down. "I know you don't want your mother running your life, but if she's busy cooking, then she can't very well be calling you every half hour and nagging you, right?"

"Okay, okay. I'll call my mother with your suggestion. But you contact me the minute there's any problem with Mitch."

"Promise." Molly hung up.

"Is this guy a dweeb or what?" Angie asked when Molly feigned pulling out her red curls by the roots.

"No he's not a dweeb, just impossible."

"Aren't all bosses?" Angie said, seeing hers approaching.

Molly chuckled, then winked. "Peter Ketteridge does have one asset to recommend him."

"What's that?"

"He wears glasses...."

THE HEADACHE that had begun during Peter's phone call worsened.

The bursts of cheering and hooting from the crew members, urging Mitch on with his skateboarding acrobatics weren't helping matters any. Along with the pounding in her head, a sense of dread enveloped Molly. It was bad enough that Mitch insisted on skateboarding between takes, but what made things worse was the fact that Mitch seemed to possess the same daredevil streak his twin brother Matthew had had—a daredevil streak that had made Matthew Marlow the premier racer of his time, but that had also snuffed out his life.

As she watched, it didn't escape Molly's notice that each trick Mitch did had to be a little more daring than the one that preceded it. She had warned Mitch he could be hurt by his reckless antics, but he'd shrugged off her warning.

"Heck, Red," he'd said, "I've been skateboarding since I was a kid, and I've gotten worse scratches from a woman."

She hadn't responded to his baiting. Instead she fumed quietly while Peter's phone call niggled at the back of her mind.

There was no use in kidding herself. Mitch had no intention of keeping his promise to her to stay out of trouble for the rest of the shoot. He was highly intelligent and just as determined to have his way. More than pure luck had gotten him his standing in the film community. Though he had a certain, well-deserved reputation, he was respected. He'd chosen each of his roles very carefully, unlike many of his contemporaries, whose promising careers had fizzled early due to ego, greed and immaturity.

Mitch and his brother had grown up in a series of foster homes, she knew. Being the only constant in each other's lives, possessing the special bond that twins share, had made Matthew's death an almost mortal blow.

Now the only communicating Mitch did was through his acting. His most intimate contact was with the camera. She didn't want to think what would happen to him if he lost that, as well.

Watching him, she saw what all women saw, and was just as susceptible to it. He was tough, emotionally wounded, gorgeous . . . and slouched and unshaven, in a pair of torn jeans. She wanted to comfort him, but he didn't want her comfort. He wanted her to leave him the hell alone. He'd told her so.

The press had labeled Mitch a control freak. Though he had a somewhat combative-compulsive personality with traits of perfectionism, workaholic tendencies, and an inability to trust others, Molly felt his wanting control wasn't just ego, as the press implied. He merely wanted to be the best. Just like Matthew.

He was terrified of being vulnerable, she surmised. But wasn't everyone? Everyone who wasn't perfect, for sure.

Was Mitch the type of man who wanted a woman like Madonna, or the character Linda Hamilton had played in *Terminator II*? she wondered. Sometimes she got the impression he preferred a woman with soft, comforting curves. Was it only wishful thinking on her part?

He had a perfect athlete's body, lithe and lean. Mitch did his own dangerous stunts in his films, despite the studio's jitters. He had even learned to ride a horse for *Jesse*.

He was sexy because he had a great sense of who he was—at least he'd had it before Matthew died. Maybe he was going to snap out of it. Molly could be worrying needlessly about him. A few more weeks of filming, and she'd have the agent's job she craved, while Mitch would have a monster hit on his hands.

Maybe, just maybe, everything would turn out all right.

No sooner had she allowed that soothing thought to surface than she heard Mitch swear. She looked up—to see him take a really nasty spill from the skateboard.

Bolting from her chair, she rushed to him, along with the other crew members. The director looked pale.

"Mitch! Are you all right?" she demanded, dropping to her knees beside him.

"Yeah, yeah, Red. It'd take more than a little tumble to . . ." He sat up, dusted himself off and started to rise. " . . . put me out of commission. Ahh . . . ouch!" He sat down again and grimaced.

"What is it? What's wrong?" Molly asked, the dread she'd felt earlier returning with full force.

Tipping back his cowboy hat, which had stayed on despite his tumble, Mitch grinned at her sheepishly.

"Don't yell, but I think maybe I broke something, Red."

That boyish grin. If she wasn't careful, Mitch Marlow was going to break more than his ankle—he was going to break her heart. If she didn't kill him first.

5

MITCH WAS AFRAID Molly would read him the riot act on the long drive back from the hospital, and he was right. He let her angry words drift over him.

After he'd fallen off the skateboard, she had managed to convince the crew and a very nervous director that it would be better if she drove him to the hospital. Her reasoning had been sound. If he'd shown up with an entourage, it would have caused a stir. Sneaking him into the hospital had been easy enough.

However, once he'd registered, word had leaked out to the mostly female staff. Thereafter, everything had taken an extraordinary length of time, requiring just about everyone to stroll through the examining room.

Each time his charming facade slipped, Molly had been there to remind him that he was acting like a child, a poorly behaved one, at that. Several sets of X rays were taken, from different angles, X rays that would no doubt surface in some celebrity auction one day. Nothing to do with a public figure was sacred. A good thing he hadn't been in for a vasectomy, he thought ruefully.

As things turned out, fortune had been with him. He hadn't broken any bones. But he had torn some ligaments in his ankle and would have to stay off it for a day or two.

He shifted uncomfortably in the front seat of the rented car. He'd pushed the seat back as far as it would go and propped his bandaged foot on the dashboard. The doctor had told him to keep it elevated and to use ice to bring the swelling down.

Pretending to be listening contritely, he took a good look at Molly. She was furious, there could be no doubt about that. The pale skin beneath the freckles that were sprinkled across her nose was flushed. As she talked, her red curls bounced emphatically and her hands gripped the steering wheel as if she were choking him.

They passed a yellow sign indicating dangerous curves, and he thought that an apt description of Molly's sweet body. Her short, black skirt, though very fashionable, was just a bit tight. One or two tiny freckles accented the smoothly rounded shoulder that had escaped her gray knit top.

All he wanted to do at that moment was lay his head in her lap. Bad idea, Marlow, he reminded himself. If he did that, he'd be needing another ice pack . . . and not for his swollen ankle, either.

"What are you thinking?" Molly asked as she glanced at him.

"Huh? Ahh . . ."

"You were smiling," she said accusingly. "I don't appreciate your attitude, Mitch. This could be serious. The studio brass are not going to think favorably about this, and I don't have to tell you Peter is going to be livid when he hears."

"So don't tell them. Look, Molly, I think you're overreacting. I hardly believe spraining my ankle is going to make the cover of the *International Intruder.*"

"No, but it will shut down production of the film, and that will make the columns and be fodder for the bean counters at the studio."

Mitch decided to change the subject. He didn't want to argue with Molly. "Let's listen to some music." Fiddling with the buttons, he tuned in Billy Ray Cyrus's monster crossover hit, "Achy Breaky Heart."

The catchy song was followed by a report of a three-car pileup blocking Highway 44 and a thirty-second, local weather update.

"Did you hear that, Red?"

"You mean about the accident? What? Are we going to get caught in a traffic jam?"

"No, I think the accident is farther south. I was referring to the local weather forecast. Maybe if we're real lucky, the rain will turn into a monsoon and we'll be able to put the blame for the shutdown of production on the rain."

"I couldn't be that lucky," Molly grumbled.

"Well, maybe I could," Mitch said. "Especially if I hedge my bet." Reaching over, he tousled the soft cloud of red curls that framed her face. His hand lingered; he waited for her reaction.

As he suspected, it was prickly.

Molly tilted her head away. "What are you doing?"

"Surely you've heard it's supposed to be good luck to run your hands through red hair."

"Not through mine, it ain't," she warned, slapping his hand away.

Matthew would have liked her. The thought came to Mitch unbidden. One of the unnerving things about life since his twin's death was reaching for the phone to call him, wanting to discuss something...someone with him. Someone like Molly. He was beginning to get over the numb feeling of shock. He'd stopped tearing up at the oddest moments. He could even bear the scent of flowers again. There'd been so many bouquets at the funeral, the sweet, sickly scent had stayed with him for days. He was even getting over the rage.

All that had been replaced by an ache deep inside.

He was ready to be comforted, and here he was, stuck with a woman who'd rather slap him up side the head than hold him in her arms and make him feel whole again, if that was even possible.

Yeah, Matthew would have liked her. Would have liked even more the trouble she was giving him. His twin had always said Mitch had a junk-food appetite for women, but that once he had a gourmet experience, he'd be a goner.

Trouble was, he didn't know if Molly Hill, with her soft curves and hard words, was a gourmet experience or a bad case of food poisoning.

"Know any more fairy tales about redheads?" Molly said, interrupting his thoughts.

"I think there's one about dreaming of a beautiful redhead bringing unexpected news, but most of what I know about redheaded women comes from the comics."

"Thanks a lot."

"Well, I don't know. . . . Brenda Starr and Jessica Rabbit aren't too shabby. And seems I recall Charlie Brown had an ongoing thing for a little, red-headed girl."

Fat droplets of rain began plopping onto the windshield. "Look, it's starting to rain. For once it looks like the weather forecasters were right. Maybe I should try running my hand through your hair again to encourage torrential downpours."

"Maybe you shouldn't," she countered. "Why don't you busy your hands with finding another radio station? That one is getting static and beginning to fade out."

Mitch turned off the radio, then groaned as he adjusted the ice pack on his ankle.

"How's the swelling?"

"My foot looks like a football and it's throbbing."

"I could say I told you so."

"Don't."

"Why'd you turn the radio off?"

"I want to try something out on you."

"What?" she asked suspiciously, looking at his hands.

"I've been playing with some lyrics for the theme song for *Jesse*. Just listen and tell me what you think, okay?" He was uncertain about it because he knew everyone was expecting a love song.

His song was about brothers—Frank and Jesse James.

He tried to keep his voice steady as he sang. The lyrics meant a lot to him; they were about two brothers, one of whom is killed. Molly's reaction was really important; he knew instinctively that she would tell him the truth, not just what he wanted to hear.

When he finished singing, Molly remained quiet.

"You didn't like it," he said, expelling the breath he'd been holding while he waited for her reaction.

He turned to look at her—and saw tears. "You're crying...."

"The song is about you and Matthew, isn't it? How can you not cry, too?"

He turned away and stared out the window. The rain was coming down in sheets. "I just can't."

THE RAIN CONTINUED its steady onslaught the next day and was blamed for the production shutdown. Molly had caught the weather forecast with her morning Danish, and as rain was predicted for several days, she'd lied and told the director Mitch was ready to film immediately.

Finishing her coffee, she decided she should at least look in on her charge. True, he wasn't going anywhere, but having him immobile and at her mercy appealed to her. As a nurse, she'd be his worst nightmare.

She was just considering what to wear when she looked out the kitchen window and caught sight of Heather Simms entering Mitch's trailer. Heather, she noticed, hadn't had any trouble deciding what to wear—a crop top and second-skin leggings. She was the perfect picture of sexy, pink innocence. Innocence was something redheads could never pull off. After all, they had a reputation for being spitfires.

Now what was she going to do? Molly wondered. She certainly couldn't go barging in on the two of them like some jealous wife. It would look as if she was snooping. She wasn't about to give him the satisfaction of suggesting any such thing.

Maybe it was a perfectly innocent visit on Heather's part. She could be borrowing a cup of sugar or something neighborly like that. Or she could be bringing Mitch some chicken soup, canned, of course.

"Yeah, right. And I'm the Princess of Monaco," Molly mumbled.

She went into the bathroom to brush her teeth and looked into the mirror. "Admit it, girl, you're jealous. No matter what size two Heather does, it's going to make you feel insecure. It's not Heather, it's you. Get a life, girl."

Taking her own good advice, she pulled on a cotton sweater and jeans, then headed out to entertain herself, in spite of the rain. Anything was better than sitting here, imagining what was going on in Mitch's trailer. Somehow she didn't think a bad ankle would put much of a crimp in his style. Wounded men brought out the nurturing side of women. Did Heather Simms have one? "My, don't we need a big saucer of milk," she chastised herself. Heather Simms was married, but it didn't mean she couldn't talk to another man. Molly was being patently ridiculous.

It was noon and still raining cats and snails and puppy dog tails when Molly returned from touring both the Jesse James Wax Museum and the spectacular Meramec Caverns. They must have been the perfect hideout for the James Gang, affording shelter to both men and horses in the early 1870s.

The rare colors of the unique mineral formations in the caverns were breathtaking, but the most impressive sight had been the seventy-million-year-old Stage Curtain formation that stood seventy feet high and was sixty feet wide.

But Jesse James and the caverns weren't on her mind at this moment. Mitch and Heather were.

She'd stopped by Heather's trailer on the way back and knocked on her door. There had been no answer.

This was more than a friendly little visit. The crew was going to talk. That didn't bother her as much as *whom* they were going to talk to. All she needed was a scandal between Mitch and a married woman to hit the tabloids. Didn't he have a brain in his head? Probably not, when presented with such a tempting sight as Heather Simms.

Back in her trailer, she kicked off her white leather sneakers and attacked a leftover Danish. When she'd done enough damage to her hips, she regained control of her thoughts, banishing the image of Mitch and Heather, alone and very much together.

She knew that moving water produced an environment high in negative ions; that made heavy rain give people a sexual turn-on. But she was the one who was restless, she was the one with the problem, not Mitch or Heather.

The problem must be turning her green eyes even greener, Molly reflected. If she were honest, she'd admit she was smitten. Already half in love with him before she set foot in the Midwest, it would be too easy to fall completely in love with Mitch now.

But she couldn't change herself to fit the type of woman Mitch might go for. She would never be a size two and had promised herself she'd never change to please anyone but herself. She had to remain true to her vision of who she was and wanted to be.

It had been a very hard lesson to learn, but Molly knew she'd wasted too many years, trying to fit the role of perfect daughter for her parents. They had loved her almost to death, smothering her until she couldn't breathe.

She recalled being driven to school and picked up by her mother, not allowed to participate in any athletic activities because of the potential risk. She'd studied astronomy for her father's sake, because it made him feel as if Joey wasn't completely gone from their lives. They had fulfilled her every need, with the result that she'd had to learn to do even the simplest things, once she'd graduated and was on her own. Learning to drive a car had been a major triumph—at the advanced age of twenty.

In the end playing a role hadn't worked. It had made her parents happy, but she'd been miserable. She'd only become happy when she'd given up trying to be what her parents wanted and followed her own instincts.

If there was even the slightest chance Mitch might love her, he was going to have to love her for who she was—stubborn, mouthy and flawed. But why would he be interested in her, when he literally had his pick of all the beautiful women in the country? She had to get a grip on herself.

She wasn't thinking straight. She was smart enough to know that women were hard-pressed to have a family and a career. Having both with an actor was a rank impossibility. She would have to give up her hard-won independence. Something she'd never do.

Yes, but... her little voice coaxed. *Some things are worth sacrifice.*

Realizing she was letting her libido take control, Molly forced herself to abandon the path her destructive thoughts were taking.

She was eyeing the last Danish when a knock sounded on the door and someone called that she had a call from L.A. Slipping her sneakers back on, she went to take the call. Was this just Peter's paranoia checking up? Or had he somehow heard about Mitch's fall from the skateboard?"

"Hello, Mr. Ketteridge."

"Tell me filming is ahead of schedule," he barked.

"Sorry to disappoint you, but it's not."

"How is filming going?" He didn't sound pleased.

"Well, if you must know, production is presently shut down."

"What! What's going on? Why haven't you called me?"

"Don't get all excited, sir, it's not Mitch's fault this time. I can't do anything about the weather. We're having driving rainstorms here, and it's predicted to rain for several days."

"You wouldn't lie to me, would you, Ms. Hill? Where's Mitch?"

"Mitch? He's still in bed, I guess."

"Do you know what time it is?"

"Yes, I know what time it is." She shook off the image of Mitch lying naked in bed. "He hasn't left his trailer, so he can't be getting into any trouble."

"I want you keeping an eye on him to see that he doesn't."

"Will you quit worrying, Mr. Ketteridge. I have everything under control," she lied.

Peter Ketteridge's next words had her suppressing a laugh. "Your idea about keeping my mother busy backfired. Do you know she's making me come to dinner every night to eat the recipes she's test-cooked?"

"Think of it as a good way to save money on expensive dinners out. With the money you save, you can afford to maintain your temperamental sports car." It amused her no end that a powerful man like Peter Ketteridge couldn't control his determined little slip of a mother.

"Don't talk about my car—my mother's gotten involved with it now, too."

"Good, then she did find a mechanic for you."

"I'm glad you think it's good. I'm appalled."

"Why? What's wrong with the mechanic your mother picked out?"

"She picked out a woman," Peter said with a heavy sigh.

"So . . ."

"A *single* woman mechanic."

This time Molly's laugh escaped. "Are you telling me that the next time you call, it might be to announce your engagement?"

"I am not amused, Ms. Hill."

"Sorry, sir."

"I keep telling my mother I have no intention of marrying anytime soon. Why won't she listen?"

"I don't know. I keep telling my mother the same thing. I guess it's not what mothers want to hear from their only children."

"What's new otherwise?" Peter asked.

"You tell me. I'm the one stuck out in the boonies, without the niceties of civilization like *Variety* and *Hollywood Reporter*. How did *Unexpected*

Pleasures do, by the way?" Molly asked. Peter's pet project had just opened.

"It grossed $10.4 million."

"I guess your star director is flying high—and so is his new asking price."

"I hope *Jesse* does as well."

"Don't worry, it will. I'm willing to bet it will blow the lid off previous grosses for Mitch Marlow films. All it needs is a really good trailer to go with the theme song Mitch wrote."

"How do you know about the theme song?"

"He sang it for me the other night. It's beautiful." She didn't mention it wasn't the love song everyone was expecting.

"I told you not to go and get personally involved, Ms. Hill."

"I'm not. I told you I wouldn't, didn't I?"

"Then how come he's singing you love songs?"

Molly took a deep breath. "He only sang it for me because he wanted my opinion, and he figured I would tell him the truth if it stank. What's that noise?"

"Alka-Seltzer fizzing in mineral water."

"Whoa, you need to relax. I've got an idea. Why don't you get tickets to a Lakers' game? You can go relax and make your mother happy at the same time."

"Would you explain to me how my going to a Lakers' game is going to make my mother happy?"

"I was thinking you could take that single lady mechanic your mother found for you."

Peter Ketteridge hung up.

DASHING THROUGH the raindrops, she passed Angie on the way back to their trailer.

"Hey, you didn't happen to see Heather, did you?" she asked. Angie was polishing off the last Danish, licking the crumbs from her fingers.

"As a matter of fact, I did see her when I headed over here. She was leaving Mitch's trailer. You want me to tell her you're looking for her?"

"No. No, that's okay. Look, we're both getting soaked. I'll catch you later, okay?"

Angie nodded and continued on her way while Molly headed for Mitch's trailer.

She didn't have any idea what she was going to say to him. How was she going to warn him about spending time alone in his trailer with Heather without appearing to be jealous? But all jealousy aside, her main concern was keeping him out of the tabloids.

Reaching his trailer, she knocked.

"It's open," he yelled.

She went inside, but he wasn't in the living area.

"Come on back."

Molly hesitated only a moment, then followed the sound of Mitch's voice to the bedroom in back.

"Are you decent?" she called as she approached.

"Which answer will get you back here?" he countered, his voice a deep growl.

"Are you covered up?" she persisted, waiting for his reply. She wasn't prudish or likely to be shocked by the sight of a naked man. She just didn't want to encourage her lustful impulses.

"I'm covered up, Red," he assured her.

Shaking her head, Molly went into the small bedroom. Mitch was lying in bed, his leg propped on a stack of pillows. A sheet covered him—sort of. It was draped across his groin and uninjured leg.

The daring look in his eyes telegraphed a signal that it was the only thing covering him. So, of course, that was the only place her eyes wanted to look. With a supreme effort of willpower she forced her gaze toward his face. It wasn't exactly a turn-off.

His blond hair was mussed. Had Heather mussed it? The ghost of a golden beard shadowed his lean jaw, and his blue eyes were laughing at her. Damn him.

"Do you really think this is such a good idea?" she asked.

"What?" He made a stab at innocence, but it went wide of the mark.

"You know what. Entertaining women in your bedroom."

"You want me to entertain you?"

"What I want is . . ." Her eyes strayed for a second to his bare chest, perfectly squared and honed. "Ah, I want you to stop entertaining women in your trailer, period." She held his gaze as she made her point. "Most especially married women."

Mitch ran his hand through his tresses. "Oh, I get it now. This is about Heather, isn't it? I can't believe it, Red. Why, you're jealous of her, aren't you?"

"*I am not...*"Molly felt her face flame, heard the shrill tone of her voice and finished softly. " . . . jealous of Heather Simms."

"You're not?" He didn't look at all convinced. "Then what's this all about? I assumed, because you found out Heather spent the morning in my trailer, you—"

"She's married, Mitch."

"I know that."

"Then you must also know your spending time, ensconced in your trailer with a married woman, is just the sort of juicy gossip the *International Intruder* is looking for."

"Looking for? Grow up, Red. These tabloid reporters don't look for stories like that to check out. They just make up whatever they think will sell copies that week."

"Like they made up that revealing photo of you and that woman nude cliff diving. The photo that got you a baby-sitter."

Mitch shrugged. "They only make up photographs sometimes. They usually go through people's garbage and put bits and scraps together to come up with more garbage. Your trouble is you worry too much. Besides, Heather's visit was perfectly innocent."

"Innocent, with you dressed like that?"

"If you must know, I had a robe on. I got undressed to get some sleep. Heather woke me up pretty early this morning, and I didn't get much sleep, what with my ankle throbbing all night."

Molly sidestepped his ploy for sympathy. "What did Heather want?"

"It's really none of your business. You're my baby-sitter, not my mother. But if it will make you happy, I'll tell you." He paused for effect. "She wanted to talk."

"Talk? About what?"

"Boy, you just don't quit, do you?"

Molly waited.

"Okay, okay. She's nervous about her first big screen kiss."

"If you ask me, there's something else I'd be more concerned about, if I were you."

"What's that? Your telling Peter?"

"No. That someone else is going to tell Sonny Simms about these practice sessions."

"Come on, Red, Sonny is a professional wrestler. He knows this is just business."

"Know what I think, Mitch. I think you're too chicken to kill yourself, and you want Sonny Simms to do it for you."

6

Fuming, Molly walked away from the rain-streaked window. "On top of that, this appears to be one of those forty-day and forty-night rains."

Angie looked up; she lay sprawled on the love seat in the living area of the small trailer the two women were sharing. In her lap was a crossword puzzle, and she was tapping a pen against her front teeth as she pondered a word. Acknowledging Molly's distress, she asked teasingly, "What do you think they're doing over there? Drawing up plans for an ark, perhaps?"

"Hardly. And if you don't mind, I'm trying not to think about what they're doing," Molly said glumly, dipping a chocolate cookie into her morning coffee. "I had hoped my little chat with Mitch yesterday would have at least some kind of dampening effect."

"Don't say damp," Angie grumbled.

Molly continued to be more worried about Heather than the weather. "Evidently Heather's appeal outweighs the very real threat of her macho professional wrestler husband tearing Mitch limb from limb." Peering over her cup of coffee, she asked, "Isn't it foolhardy to work crossword puzzles in ink?"

"Nah. It teaches me not to make mistakes, to think before I act. I've been known to have this problem with being impulsive. But even I admit it's sometimes better to act on your gut instinct. So . . . why don't you go on over to Mitch's big ol' trailer and tell Heather Simms it ain't big enough for the two of you. Throw her out on her size-two bottom. After all, you were sent here by the Ketteridge Agency to baby-sit him and keep him out of trouble."

"I can't do that."

"Why not?"

"Because it would look like I'm jealous. Mitch already implied as much yesterday. He's wrong, of course," she protested, a little too vehemently. "I plan to be one of the best agents in town. But it takes more than developing a sharp business sense. Clients need understanding. They need to be nurtured and supported. That's what the best agents give, along with their business acumen. Mitch isn't allowing me to help him at all.

"And if I fail here, I know what will happen. My parents will begin to smother me again with their concern. I'll wind up letting them talk me into being what they want for me, rather than what I want." Propping her elbows on the counter, she cupped her chin in her hand and sighed. "I can't let that happen, Angie. I just can't."

Angie inked in a word on the crossword puzzle, then looked at Molly consideringly.

"What?" Molly asked.

"You know, when you think about it, there might be something behind Mitch's actions that you haven't considered. He could be scared."

"Scared? Of what?"

"Failure."

"I haven't seen any evidence to indicate he's afraid of failure, not when you consider he's been doing his level best to sabotage his career. Besides, his career is going extremely well."

"I agree that Mitch's career is in enviable shape at the moment. But you know how this business is. Things can change overnight. The span of an acting career seems to be getting shorter and shorter. And I'm talking top-of-the-title actors, whose careers were red-hot just a film or two ago."

Molly nodded her head in agreement. "All it takes is a couple of wrong moves these days to spell disaster. So far Mitch has managed to fare better than his peers. You have to give him credit for making good choices in film roles."

"True, but remember Mitch and Matthew were very close. It's quite possible Matthew helped Mitch make those good choices. In addition to the grief of losing his brother, Mitch may be feeling worried about making choices on his own, without Matthew as a sounding board. Of course, all this is mere supposition, but it could be the real reason behind Mitch's bad attitude."

"It's possible you're right. There's also that old chestnut about being too hot not to cool down. That could be concerning Mitch, as well. He's had an incredible streak of luck at the box office."

"And he knows luck and timing play a major role in anyone's career, most especially in the arts. Maybe you ought to just cut Mitch some slack," Angie suggested.

"I guess you're right. Heather's visits could be perfectly innocent, as Mitch says."

Angie laughed, a deeply suspicious laugh. "Well, I wouldn't go that far."

"So you do think there is something going on between Heather and Mitch?"

"All I'm saying is Heather's up to something."

"Oh, that's real encouraging, Angie, just exactly what I needed to hear."

"It's not supposed to be encouraging. It's supposed to be a warning. Heather is strong and independent. Don't let her doe-eyed look fool you. She's put in her time in acting classes and she's been in a lot of failed pilots for television.

"It took a lot of doing for her to get the part in this movie. She tested several times for it before they gave it to her. I'd say Heather Simms is determined to get whatever she wants."

Molly smiled ruefully. "Sounds like Heather and I have something in common, then. I'm equally determined to get what I want. I only hope we aren't at cross-purposes."

THE REVVING of a powerful motorbike caught everyone's attention that afternoon.

Only someone crazy would be out on a motorbike in this pouring rain. It was even dangerous to ride on wet pavement, never mind mud and gravel.

Trailer doors were pushed open to see who it was. Molly was sure she wasn't the only one thinking Mitch, despite his twisted ankle, was the most likely candidate.

Instead she saw a mountain of a man, sitting astride an idling Harley-Davidson. He was dressed in enough black leather to upholster a sofa and seemed heedless of the steady rain.

She groaned, her worst fears confirmed, when the biker removed his helmet. She could kiss good-bye to her future as an agent for Ketteridge.

Sonny Simms had arrived. The scowl beneath his exaggerated, Fu Manchu mustache, didn't portend anything good. A twisted ankle was going to be the very least of Mitch's problems, if Heather was still in the trailer with him.

Sonny spotted the director. "Hey, you! You know which one of these bread boxes my wife is in?" he bellowed.

"You're?" the director asked.

Sonny looked incredulous. "You're kidding, right? No wonder you're so pale. You must live in a cave somewhere. Haven't you heard of Sonny Simms?"

The director shook his head. "No, can't say as I have."

"I'm Sonny Simms, world champion wrestler."

Sonny spied the key grip. "Hey, kid, how about you? You know where my wife's trailer is?"

"Sure thing, Mr. Simms. That's her trailer over there." The key grip pointed.

"About time someone around here knew something. I was fixin' to drown, waiting for an answer to my simple question."

Molly inched the door shut, until there was only a crack she could see through. She didn't think Sonny had seen her, and she wanted to keep things that way for now.

Sonny slapped his leather-gloved fist into the palm of his other hand. "A person would have to think there was something suspicious going on here, if they weren't a trusting sort like me. They might even give some notice to the rumors about my Heather Anne being hot for that pretty boy starring in this movie with her."

Molly's heart sank. Sonny Simms was looking for a fight—spoiling for one.

The smile beneath the mustache was menacing. "Y'all go back to what you were doing. I'm going to surprise my wife." With that he shut off the motorbike and dismounted, heading for Heather's trailer.

Molly offered up prayers that Heather was indeed in her own trailer . . . and alone.

Her prayers went unanswered.

Moments later she heard Sonny emerge from Heather's trailer. "Where's my wife?" he roared.

"She ain't in her own trailer!" Slamming the door, he made his way to the one next to Heather's.

"Is she in here with that pretty-boy actor? Is that who you're all trying to protect? Which trailer is his? Tell me!" he demanded, yanking the door open.

Molly heard him banging around inside, then watched in horror when he came back out, angrier than when he'd gone in. "I'm gonna kill that son of a bitch Marlow when I find him, if he's with my woman."

Sonny approached the next trailer and continued his jealous search. No one said a word.

Molly didn't allow herself time to think. As soon as she saw Sonny enter the next trailer, she made a mad dash for Mitch's.

Not bothering to knock, she pulled open the door and rushed inside.

The living area was empty. The television set was off. Molly hastily surveyed the area for any sign of Heather's clothing and breathed a small sigh of relief when she didn't spot any.

"Mitch, are you here?" she called, hurrying back to the bedroom area.

When she was met with no reply, she ventured into his bedroom, forcing herself not to close her eyes. She had a good reason for walking in on him—or them.

He was asleep.

Naked.

And, what was most important, alone.

She had to act fast. There was no time to appreciate the golden perfection of his body.

Though she knew what she was about to do was far above and beyond the call of duty, she had to protect him. Just being alone didn't mean he was safe from Sonny Simms's jealous rage.

"Don't think, just do it," she muttered, summoning her nerve. Time was of the essence. Her fingers fumbled with the buttons of her shirt, her nerves slowed her down as she discarded her clothes. Kicking off her shoes, she stepped out of her matching lace bra and panties. Mussing her hair, she took a deep breath and climbed into bed with Mitch. Her heart was pounding as she pulled the discarded sheet over the two of them.

Mitch mumbled some endearment in his sleep and flung one arm and his uninjured leg over her, pinning her in place. His breath fluttered softly at her neck, a warm, sensuous caress. She smelled the faint scent of a designer cologne on his skin. The fine body hair of his leg tickled her smooth skin, making it flush.

But most disturbing was his penis, suddenly alert and hard against her belly.

It was just there. Mitch continued sleeping, while his body acknowledged her. She closed her eyes, her throat tight. Mitch might live through this, but she was going to die. All her movie-house fantasies were coming true.

Right on cue there was an insistent pounding on the door. "Come on out here, pretty boy, or I'm coming in to get you!" Sonny Simms threatened.

Still asleep, Mitch didn't answer. He must have taken a painkiller for his ankle that knocked him out.

The trailer door opened with a bang and Sonny barged in with Heather in tow. She didn't look the least bit embarrassed by Sonny's macho posturing. In fact, she seemed to be enjoying it. Until she saw Molly.

Sonny stopped short. Heather didn't even make a stab at hiding her surprise and disappointment at finding the two of them together.

Waking at the commotion, Mitch sat up and blinked groggily. He looked from Sonny to Heather and then at Molly, who was very obviously naked beneath the sheet they were sharing. He said nothing.

"What's going on here?" Sonny demanded, clearly confused in spite of his aggressive posture.

Mitch looked at him. "You tell me," he said, yawning with supreme indifference.

"What do you two think you're doing, barging in on us like this?" Molly complained, playing the surprised lover.

"Who are you?" Sonny demanded.

"She's my agent," Mitch answered matter-of-factly as Molly tugged the sheet under her chin.

"You sleep with your agent?" Sonny asked.

"I think you should leave," Molly said, flinging her arm out to point the way. "Who Mitch sleeps with is hardly any concern of yours."

"It is if it's my wife," Sonny insisted.

Molly didn't know what came over her; she couldn't believe the words that tumbled from her lips. "Sonny, I can assure you that Mitch here has almost more women than he can handle. Isn't that right, honey?" She ran her finger seductively down Mitch's jaw, wondering where she'd found the nerve. "And you know those rumors about all us redheads being spitfires?" She shook her mop of red curls for emphasis and informed Sonny, "It's true. I don't think you need to be worrying about Mitch sleeping with your wife, because if he were to try such a stunt, he'd find himself singing soprano permanently."

Mitch winced. "So now you know. My agent is a shark, and I'm way more afraid of her than I am of you." Molly thought his performance worthy of an Oscar nomination.

Behaving more than hospitably, Mitch reached out his hand, offering to shake. "Nice to meet you, Sonny. Now, if you don't mind . . ." He turned to Molly and gave her a look that would have melted steel. "Molly and I were kinda busy."

"Oh. Ah. Sure." Sonny ushered out a pouting Heather.

Mitch kept Molly where she was with a warning look until they heard the sound of the trailer door closing.

Molly then began to inch her way out of bed, dragging the sheet with her.

"What do you think you're doing?" Mitch demanded.

"Leaving."

He shook his head. "Wrong."

"Look, I can explain," Molly said, reaching gingerly for her discarded clothing.

"I'm listening."

"This isn't what it looks like."

Mitch waited patiently.

"Really, I was only trying to—"

"Have your way with me while I was asleep? Shame on you, Molly. What would Peter say? Anyway, all you had to do was ask. I would have done the gentlemanly thing and obliged."

"Listen, Jerkface—"

"You sure weren't lying about that temper of yours, Red." He let his gaze travel slowly over her sheet-draped curves. "A spitfire, you say?" he taunted.

Molly looked around for something to throw besides a soft pillow and saw nothing within reach. "Look," she fumed. "I did what I did to protect you from Sonny Simms. I didn't know what else to do when he rode in here looking for blood—yours."

"He was? And you figured that by being naked in my bed, you'd distract him? Well, you certainly are distracting."

"I figured," she said, "if he found the two of us together in an intimate setting, he'd more likely believe you weren't sleeping with his wife."

"I'm not sleeping with Heather."

"Good."

"I'm sleeping with you," he said, tugging at the sheet, beneath which she was covertly trying to don her clothes. "Haven't you heard? I'm sure the news must have spread all over by now. In fact, I wouldn't be half surprised to wake up in the morning and read about us in the *International Intruder.*"

"Will you stop!" Snapping her jeans, she dropped the sheet. She glared at his frank appraisal as her lace bra disappeared under the oversize T-shirt she pulled on and knotted to one side. "I'm leaving now."

"Not a good idea," Mitch said, putting his ankle upon a stack of pillows.

"What?"

"Think about it, Molly. You've got to follow through. It's important we make what you started believable. If you leave now, he'll know he's been had."

"How—how exactly do you suggest we make this believable?" Molly stammered, eyeing him suspiciously.

Mitch rubbed his bare chest while he considered her question. Finally he said, "You ever hear Bonnie Raitt's song, 'Something to Talk about'?"

Molly nodded.

"I think that's the action we ought to take. We've got to give 'em something to talk about."

"You're suggesting . . ."

"Love bites."

"Love bites?"

"Yeah, you know, hickeys. All you have to do is offer up your pretty neck, my sweet."

She shook her head. "No." But Mitch was right. They would have to continue the charade of being lovers.

Unfortunately, it was a role she found far too easy to play.

7

THE RINGING of the telephone jarred Mitch from a restless sleep. He flung out his arm in the dark, knocking the portable set to the floor. Lunging to catch it, he banged his injured ankle, swore and despite his groggy state, located the upended receiver where it had landed on the floor.

"Hello..." he mumbled, massaging his ankle and wondering if there was any ice to put on it. He squinted at the travel clock beside his bed.

"Peter, do you know what time it is?" Mitch grumbled into the receiver.

"It's still early. Don't tell me you're in bed at one o'clock."

"It's not still early, and it's not one o'clock, either. You're calling the Midwest, where people go to bed with the chickens and where it's two hours later than it is in California. It's three o'clock in the morning here."

"Did I just hear you groan?" Peter asked.

Mitch finished propping up his throbbing ankle with a pillow. "It's nothing. I just banged my ankle when I dropped the phone. Now, what was it you wanted? Did Tom Cruise turn down $13 million to herd sheep in Australia with his wife or something and they're offering the deal to me?"

"I'm looking for Molly. She's not in her trailer."

"I know. She's right here with me."

"Damn it, Marlow, it's three in the morning."

"You want me to wake her?"

"Put her on," Peter growled.

Mitch looked at Molly, who lay asleep on the other side of the bed—way on the other side—fully clothed. He hadn't been able to talk her into a few love bites, but had made her see the sense of spending the night in his trailer.

Turning on the light, he shook her arm gently to wake her.

She continued to snore softly.

He shook her again a little harder, calling her name.

She blinked her eyes open; they were a deep, murky green from sleep. "Where—what?" she asked, disoriented.

"Peter's on the phone. Says he needs to talk to you."

"You didn't tell him I was here!"

Mitch nodded, gave her a wicked smile and handed her the phone.

"Mr. Ketteridge?" Molly spoke uncertainly, realized she had the receiver upside down and righted it. Rubbing her eyes, she yawned and shot Mitch a puzzled, *How did I get here?* look.

"I thought you promised not to have an affair with Marlow."

"I'm *not* having an affair with a client," she denied emphatically.

"Careful, Red, you'll ruin my bad reputation," Mitch said behind her.

"Is that a fact, Ms. Hill? Then you won't mind explaining what you're doing in Marlow's trailer at three in the morning."

"What am I doing in Mitch's trailer at three in the morning?" she repeated, looking at Mitch for a clue.

He mouthed a name—*Sonny Simms.*

Light dawned and she was fully awake. "I'm here, baby-sitting Mitch, what you sent me to do. Saving his life, actually."

"You're sleeping with Marlow to save his life? Really, Ms. Hill, what line did he feed you?"

Molly ignored the sarcasm and plunged right in with her explanation. "You've heard of Sonny Simms...."

"Yeah, the one with hands like hams," she said in response to Peter's apt description. "Well, Sonny boy showed up here with murder in his eyes. He was determined to find out if his wife Heather was having an affair with Mitch. I sort of averted the bloodshed by saying I was the one involved. That's why I'm spending the night in his trailer."

"Get your things—" Peter began.

"You can't fire me! I'm not—"

"I'm not firing you. I want you to move into Marlow's trailer and stay there with him until the film wraps."

"You can't be serious."

"I'm dead serious. This Simms guy is a fruit-cake. He can ruin everything. Don't you read the front page of the *International Intruder?* He and his wife are always battling over her wandering eye and his jealous rages. I don't want Marlow in the mid-dle of one of their infamous spats."

Dread—and excitement—consumed Molly as she listened to her boss's reasoning. She was going to have to move in with Mitch for the duration of filming. It was nothing less than a direct order.

"Okay, okay, I'll do it if I absolutely must."

She heard Mitch mumble something about a live-in baby-sitter and turned to glare at him.

"Why were you calling, Mr. Ketteridge?"

"I almost forgot. Are you the one who retyped my entire Rolodex?"

"Yes, why?"

"Because I don't know any Robert Abernathy at the Healing Center, yet I have a card on my Rolodex for him."

"Why are you in your office, looking at your Rolodex at one in the morning?"

"It's all your fault—yours and my mother's!"

"I don't understand."

"You were the one who suggested I get tickets to a Lakers' game to relax."

"Right. Did you have a relaxing time?"

"No."

"Why not?"

"I believe it was you who suggested I take the mechanic my mother found for my temperamental car."

"That's right. Didn't that work out?"

"Hardly. She turned out to be a Lakers' fan—a fanatical Lakers' fan. She threw her drink on another fan, starting a brawl that got us ejected from the game."

Molly's hand flew to cover her lips to silence her laugh.

"What? What?" Mitch inquired in a stage whisper, his curiosity getting the better of him, while Molly tried to keep him quiet.

"I can never go back to a Lakers' game," Peter groused.

"Really, you were that embarrassed, Mr. Ketteridge? Maybe you should look up that therapist. Abernathy, wasn't it? He might be able to get you to relax."

"Don't worry about me. You just move your things in with Marlow."

"Okay, I have everything under control." She was getting good at lying.

"Even the weather?"

"Well, maybe not the rain. But production should be starting back soon. It has to stop raining sometime."

SHE WOULD LOSE HER MIND, Molly was sure of it. She couldn't continue to live with Mitch at such close quarters and not do something patently foolish.

Only one day had passed, and already she was climbing the walls. Angie had helped her move her stuff earlier, and since then the rain had kept everyone in their own trailers. She'd tried to stay busy reading scripts Peter had sent her, but Mitch wanted to play games instead. She'd suggested he get together with the crew for some poker, but he'd said he was tired of playing poker for money and inquired if she knew how to play strip poker.

He couldn't help but know the effect he had on her, that he had, in fact, on any breathing woman. But for some reason he was enjoying using that knowledge to aggravate the hell out of her.

His campaign to disturb and distract her from her baby-sitting job was going much better than hers to teach him some good sense. She didn't think good sense and Mitch Marlow were ever going to be on handshaking terms. He enjoyed pushing the envelope too much. And for no reason other than the pure joy of doing it.

If the truth were told, Molly knew she wasn't all that much different. That was the problem. She understood Mitch way too well. And sympathized with him. Not about the foolish chances he took that would sooner or later get him killed. No, what she sympathized with was his loneliness.

All the beautiful women in the world didn't necessarily chase away the loneliness. Not if you were lonely for a particular person.

She had to stop letting Mitch get to her. In their game of cat and mouse she was very definitely the mouse. The trouble was, Mitch had some very tempting cheese as bait.

Nonetheless, no woman in her right mind would want a permanent relationship with an actor, she reflected. In fact, she wasn't sure that wasn't an oxymoron.

Molly also knew she'd never recover from a brief affair with Mitch. He wasn't serious. He was only enjoying taunting her with the idea, because she'd had the nerve to agree to baby-sit him for Peter. Turning up the heat was only his latest game.

If she played, she'd lose.

MITCH SLOUCHED on the sofa, lighted a cigarette and inhaled. His blue eyes gazed at her defiantly, he exhaled slowly and the smoke drifted around him. Sitting there in a sleeveless, white T-shirt and second-skin biker shorts, he looked like a forbidden fantasy.

"Do you have to smoke?" she nagged as she did each and every time he lighted up.

Mitch groaned and closed his eyes. "Look, I'm going to quit. Okay?"

"When?"

"I don't know. Soon."

"If you were going to quit, you'd put out that cigarette right now."

"Don't you ever give up?" Knowing she was sensitive about her red hair and her weight, he gave in to an urge and taunted, "You know, sometimes I wish I'd been locked up with someone who was mean, lean and blond."

Molly cocked an eyebrow. "Is that a fact?"

He nodded.

"I got a news flash for you," she countered. "I *am* locked up with someone who is mean, lean and blond, and trust me, it ain't what it's cracked up to be."

"Touché."

It was her turn to play rotten. "If I had my way, I'd be locked up with someone who had more sense than a stone."

"I don't know what you're talking about, unless it's about my dating Sharon Stone. You do have this thing about blondes, don't you?" Refusing to be serious, he went on, "Is that what this is all about, Red? Are you jealous?"

"It's a wonder you can fit your ego through the door," Molly muttered, flopping sideways into a big, comfy chair. "You're being purposely obtuse. You know exactly what I'm talking about," she said, determined to get the matter of Matthew's death into the open. "I'm talking about your death wish."

"Just because I smoke an occasional cigarette, it doesn't mean I have a death wish," he said, putting out the one he'd just lighted. "It only means I have a bad habit. Don't you have any bad habits, Red?"

"I'm not talking about the cigarettes, and you well know it. They'll kill you, all right, but it will most likely take years. Your death wish is more immediate."

"I do not have a death wish."

"What you have is a classic case of denial, Mitch."

"What?"

"You're denying your reckless and dangerous behavior since Matthew's death the same way you've been denying the fact that your brother, not you, was responsible for his death. You can't bring your brother back to life by feeling guilty. I know that. You have to let him go and start to live again."

"That's easy for you to say," Mitch said, his voice bleak. "You don't know what it feels like. You don't know how it feels to have a part of you gone forever."

"I know only too well what it feels like," Molly whispered softly.

Mitch looked at her oddly.

"My older brother, Joey, died when I was ten," she explained. "He was a thrill seeker like Matthew. I idolized him. Everywhere Joey went, I tagged along . . . and he let me. I think in some way he needed my childish worship. My parents were pretty tough on him, always demanding he measure up. My love was unconditional. We were very close.

"He was always taking dares and it scared me. There wasn't anything he liked better than living on the edge. I used to beg him not to be so reckless, but he'd just laugh and muss my hair.

"He died," she said, her voice catching, "he died in a stupid, senseless way. On a bet. He was trying to swim across the river and the current was too swift. I had to stand on the far shore and watch as the current pulled him under. I had to watch Joey drown, unable to save him...." Tears escaped from her eyes and she wiped them away with the back of her hand.

"I'm sorry, Molly. I didn't know."

"Well, now you do. Don't make me watch again, unable to save you. I couldn't bear it if it happened again. This time I wouldn't survive."

"What do you want me to do?" Mitch's voice was raw with pain.

"I want you to stop. Allow yourself to feel the pain, to grieve and then to live again. Get off the suicide express."

Mitch looked at her with the expression of a recalcitrant teenager.

Molly forged ahead, determined to get through the strong, tough-guy facade to the devastated man. "Don't you see what you're doing?" she demanded.

"I'm not doing anything," he said, lighting another cigarette.

"Yes, you are. You're trying to bring Matthew back with these senseless stunts. By being him. But you're not him, Mitch. He was the thrill seeker, not you."

Frustrated, Mitch stabbed out the cigarette. "We were identical twins."

"Yes, you were twins who were close," she agreed, wondering how Mitch really could bear the loss of a reflection of himself. She couldn't show her sympathy . . . that wouldn't help Mitch. "But even though you were very close, you weren't the same person. You became an actor because you needed to express yourself in another way."

"You don't know what I need—"

"Yes, I do. You need what we all need . . . to be happy. To be happy, Mitch, you have to like yourself. Lose the self-pity."

Mitch hooted. Crossing his arms over his chest, he surveyed her so intently that she squirmed. "That's a fine thing for you to say," he declared.

"Why?" she asked, fairly sure she wasn't going to like his answer. While it was perfectly fine for her to dissect him, she wasn't open to having him critique her. She was far too vulnerable for that, despite the tough-guy mouth she used as armor.

"Well, look at you," he said.

Molly's heart sank. "What about me?"

"You talk about liking yourself, yet you have this thing about your red hair and curves." Leaning forward, he said, "You're the one who's obsessed with hipless blondes, Molly, not me."

He'd touched her trigger button and she went off. "No. It's not me who's obsessed with hipless blondes. It's the society we live in. You can't be a woman alive in this time and not feel the pressure to be thinner, not feel dissatisfied with your body, no matter what shape you were born with."

"So you're saying that being a hipless blonde would make you a happier person?"

"No, because I know perfection isn't possible. But you can't stop the effect of being bombarded every day by the media's message that being thin opens up the way to acceptable beauty as well as to personal and professional success. If you want to feel female, sexy and desired, you have to work for it—work out for it. The whole, morally superior attitude of the fitness maniacs annoys me."

"So don't listen to it," Mitch said, dismissing her qualms with a shrug.

"That's easier said than done," Molly countered. "And anyway, it won't work unless men stop listening, too. They are being conditioned just as much as women are. They are being conditioned to want one stereotype of woman instead of the wide array available."

She picked up a magazine and began flipping through it aimlessly. "Besides, it's almost impossible to tune out the message, when you're confronted with the so-called ideal everywhere you turn, from television to movies to . . . to magazines," she said. The cover showed a blonde, applying makeup in her underwear.

Mitch laughed. "Boy, you really are on a tear about this, aren't you? Why are you so upset?"

"Upset? Why am I upset? I'll tell you why. It's because the message is getting worse. It's no longer enough just to be thin. Now you have to be toned. Soft must be replaced by hard. It seems to me there is a very deliberate campaign to make the female body more male."

"Not by me."

Molly glared at him.

"Okay, let's assume for a moment you're right. Why do you suppose the culture is demanding women become less feminine?"

Molly was abruptly aware that he was actually interested in what she thought. Was this part of his line? Was it pretense? Did she dare believe he was really interested in her? *Stop it. Don't get involved. You promised Peter. You promised yourself. Just answer his question,* she told herself.

"Well, since you asked, I think the current success of women in the marketplace is scaring the hell out of men. If you make women more like men, maybe they aren't as frightening."

"I'm not scared of a real woman," Mitch said, all movie-star confidence.

"You have the sense of a stone, remember?"

He let her remark pass. "Are you saying that men should be afraid of women?"

"No, I'm saying women are starting to catch on."

"Catch on to what?"

"The fact that the beauty and body requirements imposed on women are extremely time-consuming, compared to those imposed on men. You add housework, which women still do most of, plus child care, and there is no way a woman can compete equally with a man."

Mitch folded his hands behind his head and looked at her; she saw a glint flash in his eyes. "You want to know what I think?"

She wasn't sure. "What?" she asked, nonetheless, letting curiosity win out.

"I think men have more determination. Men decide to do something and they do it. It's as simple as that."

"What a line of sexist garbage!"

"You think so? Okay, then tell me and be honest. What change would you like to make about yourself that you haven't been able to make?"

Molly shrugged, the easy answer on the tip of her tongue—and off it before she could catch herself. "Lose ten pounds."

Mitch looked surprised. "I thought you didn't buy into all that body image stuff."

"I don't. But I do love fashion and I know if I were ten pounds thinner, the kind of clothes I enjoy wearing would fit better, okay?"

Mitch grinned bigtime, his eyes twinkling. "And here I thought you were just a bad girl who enjoyed wearing her clothes on the tight side," he teased.

"Disappointed, are you?" Molly said, throwing her magazine at him.

He ducked. "Maybe just a little. Surely you know it's every guy's secret desire to be seduced by a woman who's bold enough to know what she wants. A woman who throws tradition to the winds. A woman who takes over on occasion, demanding exactly what she wants, when she wants it."

It was Molly's turn to laugh, a deep, belly laugh. "And I think you've seen too many Kathleen Turner movies," she said, shaking her head.

"Uh-uh. It's not possible to see too many Kathleen Turner movies."

"Let me get this right...." Boy, either he was good at telling a woman what she wanted to hear, or he was too good to be true! "You're saying you like a woman who is independent?"

"Sure, why not?"

She looked at him doubtfully. "Sexually independent, maybe. That I'd buy. But a totally independent woman? Nah, I don't think so. A totally independent woman would probably drive you crazy." A darn shame, too.

"Why do you say that?"

"You're a movie star. You haven't got a clue how spoiled you are."

"Spoiled?" He looked affronted.

"Yes, *spoiled*. What do you think would happen if an independent woman's working hours didn't necessarily dovetail with yours? Would you be willing to accommodate that?"

Mitch winked at her. "I might."

"Might?"

Mitch rubbed his hands on his Lycra-clad thighs. "Depends on how sexually independent she is— how adventuresome."

"You think sex is an adventure? How male of you!"

"You don't think sex should be an adventure?" he asked, sounding genuinely surprised.

"Oh, great! I'm locked up with one of the Hardy Boys," Molly said with a sigh.

"Only if you're willing to play Nancy Drew...." he countered, visibly relishing the idea.

Molly shook her head. "Sorry to disappoint you, but I'm going to change the subject back. I want to know why you asked me the question about what I'd change about myself if I could."

"Oh, yeah." It was obvious he'd been totally drawn off track by the idea of her being a bad girl. "I was about to challenge you. How about it, Molly? Are you up to going one-on-one with me?"

Oh, yes, she was more than ready to go one-on-one with him between the sheets. Her body was, her heart was. Only her head wasn't. But two against one had her saying, "Depends."

"On what?"

"On what you're talking about," Molly said suspiciously, narrowing her eyes.

"I'm talking about a little man-woman experiment."

"I thought so—and I don't think so."

"Wait. Here's the deal. I'll try to quit smoking, and you'll try to lose those pesky ten pounds you were just bemoaning having. What do you say?" he coaxed. "Let's see who succeeds by the time the movie wraps."

"No cheating," Molly insisted.

He nodded. "No cheating."

"ANGIE, DON'T YOU HAVE anything chocolate to eat at all?" Molly asked, her head stuck in Angie's tiny kitchen cabinet. She'd made a thorough search of the trailer and hadn't come up with so much as a box of Cocoa Puffs cereal while waiting for Angie to return.

"Chocolate? I thought you were on a diet. Don't you have some sort of man-woman challenge of the sexes going with Mitch, to see which sex is better at willpower and self-determination?"

"I'm going to start tomorrow. Okay? Mitch doesn't have to know. Right now I need chocolate. If I don't get chocolate, I may have to kill someone."

"Let me guess who," Angie said.

"I'll give you a hint." Molly closed the cabinet door. "He's blond, blue-eyed and famous, and his name is Mitch Marlow."

"You'll never get away with it," Angie warned with mock seriousness. "Unless, of course, you blame it on Sonny, which won't work, since he went back on the road."

"I know. So if you're really, really my friend, Angie, you'll find me some chocolate."

"Will a half-eaten pack of M&M's do?" Angie held up the rumpled packet she'd pulled from her purse.

"You've saved my life," Molly said, grabbing them. "Or you've saved his."

Tossing a handful of the colorful bits of candy-coated chocolate into her mouth, she savored the rich, melting taste on her tongue. She closed her eyes in rapture.

"For heaven's sake, Molly. You look like you're having sex . . . great sex," Angie said with a ribald laugh.

"I am. It's called safe sex."

"Unsafe being—" Angie took the pack of M&M's from her and finished it off.

"Being next door." Molly flopped onto the sofa. "Oh, Angie, you don't know what it's like, being locked up with your fantasy lover for days on end

with the romantic sound of rain on the roof, end-
lessly coaxing . . . 'Yes, yes, yes.'"

"So why don't you give in to your desires for him,
if you fancy him so? Why keep torturing yourself
with denial?"

"Come on, Angie. I'm not like Heather. I'd never
recover."

"From what?"

"From being involved with him only for the duration of the film." Molly picked up a loose sofa
pillow and hugged it.

"So who says it won't last?"

"Angie . . ."

"I'm serious."

"Trust me, he's not."

"He might be."

"Angie, he's an actor."

8

MITCH HAD DRIVEN to Stanton to get ammunition for his little war with Molly. On the return trip he was lost in reflection. The radio was off, and the windows were rolled up to keep out the steady rain. The movement of the windshield wipers accentuated his almost trancelike state as he thought about what Molly had said about Matthew's death.

She was right. He had to let go of the anger he felt over his brother's death and accept it. Only then could he proceed with his life.

The bad dreams weren't coming as frequently. He didn't wake up in a cold sweat anymore, seeing smoke billow from the wreckage of Matthew's racing car . . . didn't see Matthew's lifeless body lifted from it.

The fact that Molly had shared her own guilt over her older brother's death had been comforting. She was right; Matthew had been more of a thrill seeker than he. Mitch wondered if people like Matthew and Molly's brother Joey, who'd loved living on the edge, had ever thought about the pain they'd leave behind by their senseless risk taking.

Pulling off the highway and onto the road that led to the movie location, Mitch began to hum a melody, something he was working on for *Jesse*. Once inside the trailer, he went on humming while he unloaded the groceries he'd bought.

As he took the items out of the sack, he thought of Molly. The food he'd bought would have her crying foul. He had, of course, smoked a cigarette or two on his way back from Stanton, but Molly wouldn't know that he'd cheated while she'd stayed on her diet. He'd quit for real tomorrow.

He was just melting butter in a saucepan, its aroma wafting deliciously, when Molly entered the trailer and wrinkled her nose, sniffing the air.

"What do you think you're doing?" she demanded, stalking toward him and glaring. Now he was sliding the makings of a grilled cheese sandwich into the saucepan of melted butter with a nonchalant flourish.

"Unless I'm real mistaken, I believe I'm making myself a grilled cheese sandwich." He lifted the sizzling pan, wafting the pungent aroma under her nose. "Would you like one, too?"

"You're cheating," she accused, pushing the offering away.

"What?" he asked. Had he left a cigarette butt somewhere?

"Are you nuts? You can't cook stuff like that while I'm trying to diet off ten pounds," she said, reaching to turn off the stove. "It isn't fair, and you well know it. All you're trying to do is sabotage my diet, so you can prove your ridiculous concept that men are more determined to accomplish their goals than women."

Ignoring her snit, he turned the stove back on.

"You're the one with the ridiculous concept. I can, of course, cook whatever I want. Just because you're on a diet, it doesn't mean I have to be on one, too. I'm the one who has to quit smoking, remember?" His quiet, sensible words were followed by a sexy grin. "You do know what that means, don't you, Molly?"

"What?" she snapped.

"It means, Red, that I shall have to find something to do with my oral fixation...."

Mitch saw her flush beneath the freckles on the bridge of her nose. He knew it annoyed the hell out of her that he had the ability to make her flush at all. And he was fairly certain she wasn't used to anyone having that sort of control over her. Molly

Hill was the sort of young woman who liked to have the last word—not to be left speechless.

Molly didn't respond to his suggestion and turned to rummage in the refrigerator.

Watching her, he wondered what it would be like to leave her speechless in bed. On second thought, he decided he'd rather have her making wild, throaty sounds as he brought her to satisfaction. He raised an eyebrow at the idea. It was strange how she kept creeping into his head at the oddest moments.

At this moment, studying her backside, covered in second-skin, Lycra leggings trimmed with lace, he had a compelling urge to stroke it. To pull her back against him and nestle her against his sex.

What would she do if he acted on his impulse?

Their earlier conversation about independent women came back to him. Now that would be a change! A woman who didn't expect him to be Mitch Marlow, movie star. A woman who maybe wanted him and not his celluloid image.

He smiled, relishing the idea. Just for once, he would welcome the chance to lie back and simply enjoy. He could really go for Molly using his body as her own, personal playground.

Molly had been right. Kathleen Turner was his type of woman. Perhaps he'd been wrong to claim not to be a thrill seeker. Maybe the kind of thrill that fired his engines was the idea of having his agent really on top of things....

Molly turned from the small refrigerator, empty-handed. "I guess I'll eat the catered meal with the crew. I don't see why you can't, as well."

"Because I have special tastes," Mitch said, resisting the urge to laugh at how that sounded.

She frowned at him.

"Well, it was you who said I'm spoiled."

"Great. What am I supposed to do, then, while you're in the trailer, cooking all this mouth-watering food? Will you please tell me that?" she asked crossly.

"Oh, I've thought of that one, too," he answered, all too accommodatingly. Reaching into the grocery sack, he brought out the remaining contents; a bag of carrots and another of celery.

She took them from him, telling him beneath her breath what he could do with them. Tossing the plastic bags onto the counter, she turned back to him with a bright smile. "Tell you what," she said as he slid his grilled sandwich onto a plate. "You're such a damn fine cook, why don't you be a prince and do these up into sticks for me?"

He wiped his hands on a dishcloth and picked up the vegetables along with her challenge. "Sure thing, Red. Hey, I can be a nineties sort of man. No problem."

He knew that he was making her very nervous and was glad. While he quite liked her self-confidence, if he got her all disconcerted, he might yet tumble her into bed.

He took a bite of his grilled sandwich and finished up the carrot and celery sticks. The rain was doing its job in their dance of seduction. Its steady assault was inching up the frustration level, degree by degree.

For the moment he was content to let Molly pretend there was no electricity between them. Sooner or later he'd bed her hot body.

And then he really thought about it—thought about how difficult she could be.

Molly Hill . . . he must be suicidal!

"Hello, Mr. Ketteridge," Molly said, munching on a carrot stick.

"Do you know who Robert Abernathy is? *Do you?*"

Molly winced and took the phone away from her ear.

Mitch grinned, able to hear Peter's outrage from across the room.

Molly waited for Peter to vent his rage. He was on another one of his tears. His yelling didn't really mean anything. She knew it intimidated a lot of people, but it didn't faze her. She knew it was only part and parcel of his expansive personality. He could yell a never-ending stream of orders and then give an agent trainee tickets to a coveted event plus a free dinner.

She also knew tenacity and determination to get what you wanted were the qualities that made a good agent. They were what got you the beach house, the sports car, the prestige and the power. In a word, the success she wanted. She could learn a lot from Peter Ketteridge, and she was smart enough to know it.

Smart enough to know, too, that Hollywood had changed.

In the past the studio heads, movie stars and the producers had been the ones who held the reins of power, but no more. In the new Hollywood the power had shifted into the hands of agents. Today they packaged movies, made the money deals and controlled the careers of their clients.

Moving gingerly, Molly put the phone back to her ear and answered Peter's question.

"Yes, Robert Abernathy was the therapist I put on your Rolodex. Right?"

"Right. And I went to see him at your suggestion."

"If you went to see a therapist, why aren't you more relaxed?"

"I'll tell you why, Ms. Hill. It's because Robert Abernathy is a hydrotherapist, that's freaking why!" Peter yelled.

"But I still don't understand, Mr. Ketteridge," Molly said. "I've never heard of a hydrotherapist.

"They put the water where? You're kidding," she said when he told her.

"No, I'm not kidding. This is L.A. I don't want you putting any names on my Rolodex without checking with me first, especially ones my mother gives you. Understand?"

"Yes, yes. I understand. I take it Mr. Abernathy was your mother's idea."

"Yes, he was another of her finds," Peter said dryly. "Listen, you have any idea what could have happened to the Forster contract?"

"Isn't in the file?"

"No. Do you remember reading it?"

"Yes."

"Is Mitch there?" Peter asked.

"Yes." Molly handed over the phone.

"Planet Hollywood wants to display the bike the studio gave you from *Dangerous* in the restaurant. What do you think?" Peter asked.

"Sure, they can display it. I'm not planning on riding it anymore."

"You're not?" Peter asked, his surprise audible. "Why?"

"Oh, I'm thinking of becoming a more responsible person. I know how happy that would make you, Peter."

"I hope that's Ms. Hill's influence."

"Yeah, you could say it's Molly's influence."

"Still, I hear the film is going over budget. . . ."

"Yes, I know the film is going over budget, Peter. It's still raining, so they can't shoot. I don't think there's anyone you can take a meeting with about the rain. You have to learn to chill out, Peter. Why don't you try getting a personal trainer or something to work out the kinks?"

"I'm fine. It's you that needs taking care of. You tell Molly to call me as soon as shooting starts."

"Yeah, okay. I'll have Molly call you. But Peter, I got to tell you," Mitch said, looking at Molly. "They're bringing in chimps and parrots by the truckload. I think they may be relocating the rain forest."

He stared at the phone. "He hung up on me! The guy has no sense of humor! But then, I don't imagine I would, either, after six high colonics."

THEY COLLAPSED TOGETHER onto the sofa. The trailer, though lushly appointed, was really too small for two strangers to have their separate space. And so they were constantly in each other's. The occasional brushing touch was inevitable.

Now they were shoulder to shoulder, thigh to thigh, fitting together in an intimate and familiar way.

"Hello, Red." His voice was whisper sexy, acknowledging their closeness, acknowledging her femaleness.

Molly turned her head and thought she saw simmering, sexual desire. She caught her breath.

No. He's an actor, she reminded herself. *This is all a game to him. He can make me see whatever he wants. Most especially when it's what I already want to see.*

She jumped from the sofa, picking up the dishes and glasses from dinner and carrying them into the kitchenette.

Mitch didn't comment. Instead he asked her to bring his guitar while she was up, pleading his still tender ankle.

Feeling like a skittish schoolgirl, she brought it to him.

Still disturbed by the sensual feelings Mitch aroused in her, Molly busied herself cleaning up the kitchenette, while he began to strum the guitar, tuning it. The rich, seductive sound of his voice began to crawl over her body; he was singing the words to the new ballad he was working on for *Jesse*.

His singing further unnerved her when she focused on the lyric and found herself caught up by the words of love. She closed her eyes, allowing images of the two of them in a romantic setting to surface.

You've gotta snap out of it, she told herself, blinking her eyes open when she realized what she was doing. One thing was clear; cabin fever, plain and sensual, had set in.

Finishing in the kitchenette, she faced Mitch.

"Would you mind terribly not doing that right now?" she asked.

"You don't like it?"

"No, it's not that."

"It still needs some work," he said with a shrug, setting aside the guitar. "Speaking of work, I have a job for you, if you'll do it."

"Me?"

He nodded. "I need someone to run my lines with me. I'm having some trouble getting them down."

"I don't know...."

"Well, if you'd rather I ask Heather..."

"Where is Heather? I haven't seen her hanging around here lately."

"I think her nose is out of joint, since you aced her out as my woman...."

"Your what!"

"Well, I could ask her, if you'd prefer."

"No. I'll read lines with you," Molly said, resigning herself to the task.

While he went to the closet to get copies of the script, she tried to prepare herself for a long night. Still, she was so nervous and jumpy that a sudden clap of thunder made her scream.

Mitch came running. "What is it? What's wrong?"

"Nothing," Molly answered, embarrassed. "I saw a bug or a...mouse or something, but it's okay now. It's gone."

"A bug or a mouse? Musta been some bug."

"Do you have the script?" she asked. When had she become a dithering idiot? Did sexy, gorgeous Mitch Marlow make all women act like idiots? Or was it just her?

"Got 'em," he said, holding up the scripts. "One for each of us."

"Where do we start?" she asked, taking one from him.

"Page fifty."

Molly flipped through the script.

"Then take off your gown," Mitch read.

The way he said it made Molly want to do it. Except she wasn't wearing a gown, and she certainly wasn't acting out any love scene with him. But something about his words sounded familiar. Then she recalled the dream she'd had while reading the script—the dream in which *she* had played the starring role. . . .

"Mitch."

"That's not your line. Your line is 'What?' Go ahead, read it."

Oh, hell! He wasn't going to give up. The only thing to do was to get it over as quickly as possible and not to let him see her sweat, as the commercials said.

"Molly. . . ?"

"Okay, okay. What?" she read.

"You heard me. I said, take off your gown. I want you to scrub my back, and if you don't want to completely ruin that pretty velvet, you'd best take it off." Mitch lay back across the sofa.

"I'm *not* taking off anything." Molly's reading was perfectly in character.

"That was good," Mitch commented.

He continued reading his part. "Do I have to get out of this tub and make you, miss?" He gave her his best, Clint Eastwood-stony stare.

"No!" Molly was surprised by the energy that came naturally with the line. "No. Okay. I'll do it, but you have to promise to keep your head turned away."

"I promise," Mitch read, laughing wickedly on cue.

Searching for a prop, Molly grabbed a white dish towel and advanced toward him.

"What do you think you're doing?" he demanded, the perfect inflection in his voice as he watched Molly approach.

"Blindfolding you," Molly said. "It's in the script, remember."

"That really isn't necessary," Mitch objected.

"Uh-uh. If it's in the script, we have to follow it," Molly insisted, deciding it would be easier to read the love scene with him if he were blindfolded.

"How am I supposed to read my lines?" he wanted to know.

"Just a minute. I have a solution," Molly said, disappearing and returning a minute later with a silk scarf. "We'll use this. You can see through it, but it will still give you the feel of being blindfolded."

"You just happened to have this?" Mitch inquired, looking at her. "Have you ever done this before?"

"Shut up."

"Then I can't say my lines."

"Then read your lines, but nothing more."

Mitch looked at his script and read his next line.

"You're taking all the fun out of this."

"Not for me," she read.

"Pretend you're undressing," Mitch instructed.

"Use your imagination," Molly countered.

"Good idea," he said, way too agreeably. A provocative smile played at his lips, but he stayed in character, pretending he heard the seductive sounds of her undressing before him.

"Go on. Your line," he prompted.

"Hand me the soap," she read.

Mitch felt for the imaginary bar of soap on the sofa that had suddenly become his bathtub. Locating the soap, he held it out to her, just beyond her reach.

Sighing, Molly stepped forward, reaching for the imaginary bar.

Mitch grabbed her hand, catching her off balance, and she fell onto the sofa with him.

"Pretend you hear the water splash," he instructed.

"What do you think you're doing?" Molly sputtered.

"Exactly what you want me to, Red. . . ." Mitch knew exactly what he was doing and he knew his lines. His blindfold didn't hide her secrets from him, either. This little game had been a pretense to get her where he wanted her—where, in fact, he knew she wanted to be.

She didn't remember what happened next. Her dream had been interrupted by Angie telling her about Mitch's game of chicken.

Well, he was about to find out that chicken was a game anyone could play. It didn't always have to involve racing cars. But it always involved taking risks.

Risks like those she was about to take.

Taking a deep breath, Molly decided to lay her career, her ego and her heart on the table.

9

"WOULD YOU EXCUSE ME for a moment?" Molly asked, levering herself out of Mitch's arms.

"Wait! Where are you going?" Mitch wanted to know, looking like a kid who'd just dropped his ice-cream cone after only the first lick.

"I'll be right back," Molly assured him. "I'm going to slip into something more comfortable."

In the small bedroom she rummaged through her clothes, coming up with a long, white cotton sweater and a pair of fluffy, white cotton socks. Peeling off her Lycra leggings and matching paprika top, she pulled on the sweater and socks— nothing else. After running a brush through her tangled curls, she let the humidity have its way and went back to Mitch.

"So how comfortable did you get?" Mitch asked, reaching to remove his blindfold.

Molly stayed his hand.

"No. Leave the blindfold on."

Mitch's hand hesitated a few seconds, then returned to his side. "Ah, a bad girl, after all."

Was she a bad girl? Molly didn't know about that. But she did know that having Mitch see her through hazy silk gave her the confidence to go with her desire, to take control.

"I thought we'd talk," Molly said, aiming to disconcert him.

"Talk? Oh, no! You're going to berate me, aren't you? Isn't this going a bit too far? Peter the Terrible never blindfolds me when he berates me. Perhaps you should check with the Ketteridge Agency's manual. I really don't think this is agency policy."

"Mitch . . ."

"Oh. Were you wanting to talk about protection, then?"

"Mitch!"

"Aw, now, Molly, don't be embarrassed. I don't have a problem with using protection. You, of all people, should know that I'm not a sheathophobic by the stash you saw in my bedroom drawer."

"Judging by the supply in your bedroom drawer, I'd think you had Batman's rubber fetish, if I didn't already know you used them for water bombs," she answered sardonically.

"Okay, okay. What do you want to talk about?"

"I want to know what turns you on."

He sat bolt upright. "You *are* a reporter from the *International Intruder*. I had you pegged, right from the moment I laid eyes on you. That's why you know so much about Batman. You're one of those bloodsuckers, aren't you?"

"Mitch, I'm serious here. I really do want to know what turns you on."

"What turns you on, Molly?" His voice was resonant with suggestion.

"Uh-uh. I asked you first."

"You're absolutely certain you're not a reporter for the tabloids?" he inquired, making himself comfortable again on the sofa.

"Get real, Marlow. If I were a reporter for the tabloids, I'd hardly have stayed to baby-sit you. It's not exactly a walk in the park, you know. I would have only stayed long enough to get the information I wanted, then I'd have blown this Popsicle stand, as they say."

"Then you only want to know for your own satisfaction what turns me on. Is that right?"

"Not exactly."

"What, then?"

"I want to know for *your* satisfaction."

"Hmm . . . I do like the sound of that. Okay, let's see. I guess I'd have to put, say . . . red hair—long, wild, sexy red hair—freckles, green eyes and curves at the top of my list as turn-ons. Is that what you wanted to know?"

"Don't patronize me, Mitch."

"You've got it all wrong. You're thinking of the old Mitch Marlow."

"The old Mitch Marlow?"

"Yeah, the wild, reckless, stupidly immature one. The one without culture or class. You know, Jerk-face. What you're looking at now is the brand-new and much improved version."

"I'm supposed to buy that?"

"Why not?"

"Because you're just playing a new role. A role you fancy for the moment, because you think you can make me buy it."

"You know what you sound like, Red? You sound like a cynic. You're awfully young to be a cynic, don't you think?"

"I'm not a cynic. I'm a realist. If it walks like an actor and talks like an actor, then the odds are it's an actor."

"Come on, Red, give me a break! I'm telling you I could fall in a big way for a woman like you with a mouth that doesn't quit."

"Really? Is that what turns you on, Mitch...oral sex?"

"Why, you planning to talk me to orgasm?" he asked, baiting her again.

"Is that what you'd like?" Molly suggested, turning the tables.

"I'd like to see you do that."

"You think I can't?"

"I don't know. How's your diet coming along?"

"My diet is going just fine, despite your childish efforts to sabotage it."

He let her jab pass. "I'm glad to hear it. I have just one question for you."

"What is it?"

"Have you cheated?"

"No," she lied. Without skipping a beat, she turned the question on him. "And you? How is your campaign to quit smoking working out?"

"Fine. It's going fine."

"Have you cheated?"

"No," he lied.

Molly rubbed her hands on her bare thighs. "Sounds like what the two of us have here is a good, old-fashioned stalemate, wouldn't you say?"

"Sounds like," he said agreeably. "Unless, of course, you *can* talk me to orgasm, in which case you'd be the one to win, hands down. No pun intended."

"A bad pun, nonetheless," she couldn't help noting.

"I'm waiting. . . ."

"Okay, you're on. Without any help from you, I might add, I'm going to find out what turns you on."

"Don't get in a snit about my not being more forthcoming, Red. It'll be more interesting for both of us if you have to find out what turns me on, don't you think?"

She ignored him for a minute as she plotted their game. "When I ask you for a word, just pick one at random. Some word that appeals to you, for whatever reason. Do you understand?"

"No, but I'll humor you."

"Good. Are you comfortable?"

"Yes."

"Enjoy it, because it isn't going to last."

"It's not?"

"No. When I'm done with you, you're going to want a cigarette and you can't have one."

"I'm waiting. . . ."

"Okay, give me a word."

"What kind of word?"

"An event word."

"An event, huh?" Mitch thought for a moment, then gave her an eight-by-ten-glossy smile. "Wedding."

Molly filled her mind with images, then began fashioning the fantasy. "It's a summer wedding."

"Is it raining?"

"No."

"Good."

"The wedding is taking place outside, in a garden with a wide expanse of lawn, fishes splashing in a lily pond, and rose beds in full bloom. A large tent has been set up for the buffet."

"What kind of food?"

"What kind of food?" she repeated.

"Yeah, remember I'm blindfolded and I can't see."

"It's an early wedding, so the caterers are preparing brunch: frittatas, brown-sugared bacon, scrambled eggs whipped with cream cheese, fresh berries in cream, butter- and cinnamon-drenched French toast and ambrosia punch."

"Yeah, you're on a diet."

"Shut up."

"There are tables scattered on the lawn for the guests. Each table is festooned with ribbons, and there are candles and fresh bouquets of dewy, garden roses. The wedding is formal, so the tables are draped with soft pastel linens and set with delicate china, crystal and gleaming silver. Can you see it?" she asked the silent Mitch.

"Through a sort of silky haze," he said dreamily, surprising her.

"The musicians have taken out their instruments and are tuning up, running through the song for the wedding ceremony," she continued.

"What song are they playing?"

Molly couldn't believe how easily she'd gotten Mitch to participate, then it dawned on her that it was all part of being an actor. He needed details to visualize the scene. She couldn't admit that one song had been playing in her head, ever since she'd decided to have her way with him—a song of Cher's called, "Just like Jesse James." There was nothing better to describe either Mitch's reputation as an outlaw lover or their current, cat-and-mouse situation.

Instead she plucked something from left field, a sexy, achy old Waylon Jennings standard. "How about 'Can't Keep My Hands off of You'?"

He let out a low whistle. "Good golly, Miss Molly. You are one for getting to the point."

Molly went on. "The bride is inside, putting on her white silk organdy hat, while the groom waits impatiently in the garden, a white tulip in the lapel of his black tuxedo."

Mitch chuckled.

"What?" Molly asked, puzzled.

"An Irish setter just ran by and flopped into a flower bed to lick wedding-cake icing from his nose."

"Mitch!"

"Don't holler at me! Holler at Rover!"

Molly shook her head and smiled, then picked up the thread of her fabrication. "Meanwhile . . . the bride is pulling on her gloves and picking up her bouquet of white tulips, getting ready to join the groom for a few moments before the guests begin to arrive."

"What is the bride wearing?"

"Something simple, sophisticated . . . A lace jacket that buttons up over a cloud of full, silk organdy skirt."

"I hope she doesn't have her beautiful red hair tucked up beneath the matching hat."

"I didn't say anything about red hair."

"Trust me. The bride has red hair, green eyes, and doesn't know her string of pearls is about to break."

"Pearls . . . ?"

"Keep up, Red, we're in the garden now."

"The lilacs are blooming. Can you smell their fragrance?" she asked without skipping a beat. "Oh, but do you see what's by the ivy-covered wall?"

"You mean Rover, digging up the prize rose-bushes?"

"No. The white canvas tent set up for the wedding feast. The caterers haven't arrived yet, so the tent is empty."

"You can bet the groom has noticed the opportunity. What about the bride? Has the same thought occurred to her, or is she a bashful bride?" he teased.

"No."

"Good."

"Why do you say that?"

"Because I have an idea where she's leading the groom."

"And where might that be?"

"Astray, one hopes. She *is* planning to lead him astray, isn't she?"

"Yes."

"Finally. In that case, I have only one complaint, maybe two."

"What's that?"

"One. What took her so long? Two. Has anyone ever died of biker shorts?" he asked, trying in vain to adjust his own. "Never mind, go on...."

Molly couldn't help the thrill of satisfaction she felt at the sight of his uncomfortable state. Heady with her success, she began turning up the heat.

"The bride and groom are now inside the tent, alone, not yet married, and with the tent flaps closed."

"Scandalous. Go on. . . ."

"I think it's time for you to give me another new word before I continue."

"What sort of word?"

Molly thought for a moment. "A wedding word. Something bridal would be good."

"Something bridal..." he mused, drumming his fingers on the sofa. "I've got it. Garter."

Molly giggled. "Don't you think you're being a bit eager?"

"Hell, no! If you ask me, I think I've been bloody patient."

"But what about the caterers and wedding guests? They could arrive at any moment, you know."

"That's the thrill, isn't it? If I recall correctly, we did establish that this bride isn't bashful."

"You do like your woman to be a bit of a tart, don't you?"

"What's not to like?"

"Oh, no!"

"What? What?" Mitch demanded.

"The groom has tucked his forefinger beneath the bride's strand of antique pearls and is pulling her close for a kiss, but the string has broken, scattering the pearls in the grass."

"The groom broke the bride's necklace on purpose," Mitch informed her.

"He did?"

Mitch nodded.

"What a cad!"

"Not really. He had a good reason."

"You mean he bought a new necklace for the bride to wear?"

"Mercenary little thing, aren't we? As a matter of fact, he has. But right now he has something else on his mind."

"The garter, right?"

"That and bartering the pearls he finds in the grass at their feet."

"Bartering? For what?"

"Favors from the bride."

"Let me guess. Sexual favors?"

"You catch on fast, Red."

"What if the bride doesn't agree to the groom's blackmail?"

"She will."

"But how do you know?"

"Easy. The bride's got a bit of a mercenary streak—she'd make a great agent—and the groom has just happened to let her glimpse the velvet, jewelry box in his tuxedo pocket."

"How many pearls has the groom found?"

"Two," he answered and smiled his wicked smile.

"Only two?"

"That's all the groom needs."

"Really? It's a wonder the groom's ego fits inside the tent."

"You don't like the groom."

"Depends."

"On what?"

"On what he asks for his two favors."

"You tell me."

"Okay, I will. One, he's pulled out a chair and asked the bride to sit on his lap."

Molly moved to stand in front of Mitch.

"What are you doing?" he asked.

"Helping you get the picture," she answered. "The bride lifts her floaty, organdy skirt...." She straddled his lap, shins resting on the sofa, on either side of him. "Mmm... those biker shorts are tight," she observed as she rubbed herself against him.

Mitch's response was a strangled groan.

"Then the groom settles his hands on the bride's waist," she instructed.

Mitch moved his hands.

"On the bride's *waist*," Molly repeated until he followed her direction exactly.

"The blindfold. I misjudged...." Mitch lied.

"The bride then unbuttons her lace jacket, because it's warm."

"And the groom helps her, laying the lace jacket across the table beside them."

Molly stretched her arms high.

"Now what?" Mitch asked, feeling her move.

"The bride is waiting for the groom to slip her camisole over her head."

Moving his hands very carefully, Mitch tucked his fingers beneath the bottom edge of her long sweater and tugged it up, over her head.

"In case you're wondering, the groom's hands go back on the bride's waist," Molly said into the sensually charged silence.

"I was afraid of that," Mitch grumbled, reluctantly following her directions.

"What about the groom's mouth?" Mitch asked hopefully.

"The bride isn't ready to be kissed, not just yet."

"How about things other than kissing?"

"Such as?"

Mitch leaned forward, his warm breath brushing the shell of her ear. "Such as licking and sucking, if the bride says please," he rasped.

Molly's pulse quickened; she did his bidding. "Yes, please."

Mitch traced the full, sexy pout of her lips with his furled tongue . . . suggestively, slowly, exquisitely.

When he didn't kiss her, she felt bereft, despite her instruction not to.

He lowered his mouth to her neck and began sucking gently, giving her the hickey he'd promised her, the night she'd crawled naked into his bed to protect him. A naughty thrill stole through her.

He paused to whisper decadent suggestions of what he would do to her if only time permitted. But, alas, the guests and caterers would be there at any moment.

Escalating the pitch and fever of the moment, he moved his mouth from her neck to her breasts, sucking hard and urgently on one pearled nipple.

Her response was immediate and overwhelming. She moaned loudly and caught her breath.

He favored the other nipple with the same treatment, until the slight, aching warmth in her loins became a throbbing need.

"Please," Mitch said, his lips again at her ear, nibbling, coaxing. "Please, baby, please."

"Is this favor number two?" Molly asked.

"Yes." Now his breathing was shallow, his teeth raking her earlobe.

"Then in that case, you may kiss the bride."

"Can I take off the blindfold?"

"No."

His lips descended to devour hers in a slow, consuming caress that was a pantomime of lovemaking.

Mitch began tearing off his clothes with Molly as his eager helper. Their passion was an unstoppable force, an avalanche, a river flooding its banks, a volcano erupting. Nothing in the world could stop their desperate need.

They had to have, must have, each other.

Nothing could stop them—except the ringing telephone.

"Don't even think about answering it," Mitch warned, standing and hopping on one foot as he tried to peel off his biker shorts.

"I have to answer it, Mitch."

"No, you don't. Ouch!" He rubbed the shin he'd banged on the sofa.

"Yes, I do. It could be Peter calling."

"More the reason not to answer."

Unable both to argue with a gorgeous, naked, blindfolded man and ignore the ringing, Molly answered the phone.

Mitch was gesticulating madly, shaking his head. He was clearly wild with disbelief. His hands were making choking motions to show her how frustrated he was. Not that she couldn't draw that conclusion from the sight of the other evidence.

"Hello, Peter."

Mitch groaned and sank onto the sofa beside her.

"No, you're not interrupting anything."

It was the wrong thing to say; Mitch clearly took her words as a challenge.

He raised his hands to undo the silk scarf that covered his eyes—a gesture meant to distract and unnerve Molly; a deliberate attempt to get her off the phone.

It only half worked. It did distract and unnerve her. She tried to dissuade Mitch, shaking her head while she continued her conversation with Peter. When Mitch paid her no heed, she held her hand over the receiver and mouthed the words, *No, wait!*

Mitch's fingers toyed with the scarf, lingering on the knot; he was milking the suspense with the finesse of a practiced stripper.

"Hang up the phone," Mitch urged.

"Don't," she said out loud. "No, I didn't say anything, Peter. Great, you found the Forster contract. Where was it?"

"Hang up the phone," Mitch repeated.

Molly held up her hand, begging for five minutes, then realized Mitch couldn't see it. "Did their meeting with the new director go okay?" she asked Peter as he filled her in.

"Three . . ." Mitch began.

"Just a minute," Molly said.

"Two . . ." Mitch continued, his fingers loosening the knot.

She shook her head and went on listening to Peter.

"One," Mitch said on a note of dramatic finality.

Unknotting the blindfold, he slid the silk covering from his eyes—an act that also unveiled Molly's voluptuous, naked body.

She felt a warm, rosy flush spread over her skin at his voracious appraisal and appreciative smile.

When she looked into his eyes, she knew she was in trouble. There, in the dancing, blue depths, was a determined look of mischief, fueled by unleashed desire.

Mitch Marlow was about to be more trouble than she could handle. She had to get a grip on things. But that was hard to do when you were both naked and very distracted.

"Hello. Are you still there?" Peter asked.

"Yes, Peter, I'm still here." Trapped in a real-life and very warped version of *Peter and the Wolf*, she thought as Mitch maneuvered her sideways.

"I decided to live dangerously and get a personal trainer," Peter informed her.

"No! I don't believe it for a moment!" Molly said, squealing in disbelief.

"What?" Mitch whispered, taking her sock-clad feet into his hands.

"You really got a personal trainer?" she asked Peter, trying to ignore the fact that Mitch was removing her socks—with his teeth.

She began to squirm and had to suppress a giggle when Mitch telegraphed his intention to do his level best to get her off the phone.

"No, stop! Will you quit!"

Mitch ignored her shocked pleas and continued to lick the arch of her foot, snaking his facile tongue between her toes.

"No, not you, Peter," she explained, trying all the while to slap away Mitch's hand and mouth. But he was too agile; her efforts were to no avail. Instead he intensified the assault by nudging her knees apart.

"Is Marlow behaving himself?" Peter wanted to know.

"Yes, Mitch is behaving," she lied, nearly choking.

Mitch began kissing the insides of her knees with slow, tongue-enhanced kisses.

"You can't..." Molly said, almost swallowing her words with a gurgle.

"What did you say?" Peter asked.

"Nothing. I didn't say anything, Peter. Yes, I think it's great that the Forsters are going to pl-pl-play..." Mitch had begun to trail kisses up the insides of her thighs. "...in the Celebrity tennis event."

"Is it still raining?" Peter inquired.

Mitch's lips trailed kisses around the triangle of red curls, then moved up, over her abdomen. "Yes, Peter. It's still rai-rai-raining!" Mitch's mouth had closed possessively over one nipple.

Molly's hand flew out to tug at his long locks, trying desperately to pull his head away. It was no use, and she didn't really want him to stop.

"You know, Ms. Hill, maybe it would be a good idea to get Mitch a personal trainer. A regular workout might improve his mood."

"I don't think...I...I..." Mitch's mouth was sliding south again.

"What did you say? I can't understand what you're saying."

"I...ah...I said, Mitch's mood is...is..." His mouth closed over her sex, and he thrust his tongue inside. "Mitch!"

"What? Is something wrong?" Peter bellowed into the phone.

"No!" Molly gasped.

"Are you sure? Are you all right, Molly?" he pressed.

"Yes, I'm...I'm... I'm a little out of breath from...ah...working out."

Mitch's hand slid beneath her buttocks, raising her to him.

"What is Mitch doing?" Peter asked.

"Mitch is...he's...ah..." Molly couldn't think and closed her eyes.

Mitch's mouth grew more insistent and her breathing grew shallow.

"Are you sure you're all right?" Peter asked. "You aren't overdoing your workout, are you?"

"I'm...I'm fine," Molly assured him, her eyes flying open when she felt Mitch lever himself over her.

"What are you doing?" she demanded.

"I'm having a whirlpool for my aching muscles." Peter answered the question she'd asked Mitch.

"No, not now!" Molly cried out. "You . . . It's . . . Ahh . . ."

Mitch ignored her protest and proceeded to bury his satiny, hard sex deep inside her.

"What do you mean?" Peter asked puzzled by her words.

"Not you, Peter. I mean . . . I . . . ah . . . oh!" She saw Mitch's eyes glitter; he began to tease her speechless with a series of slow, sensuous thrusts.

"Molly . . . Molly?" Peter asked again.

Mitch took the phone from her hand. As his thrusts grew more urgent, he said, "Molly will have to call you back, Peter. *Her* personal trainer is here. Goodbye."

10

THE RAIN finally stopped. The powerful storm had scattered small branches and debris, but the day dawned with bird song. They hopped between the puddles, looking for worms, while shafts of sunlight streamed between the patches of gray cloud.

It was still too muddy to begin shooting, but during the day the sun did its job, and the ground dried out. Production could start again tomorrow. Everyone in the crew was in an upbeat mood, though they knew they'd be working straight through several weekends to bring the production back on schedule.

Mitch and Molly's lovemaking had surprised them with its Valentine sweetness. Today the trailer they shared seemed to confine them even more than usual—supplying fresh tinder for new encounters.

So when Mitch suggested the crew drive into Saint Louis for a night of fun and relaxation, everyone thought it was a good idea.

Everyone except Molly.

As far as she was concerned, it was hard enough to keep an eye on Mitch when he was on the movie set. Saint Louis offered just too many temptations.

Most of the crew, along with Angie and the key grip, were avid to try the Screaming Eagle and the Ninja roller coaster rides at Six Flags amusement park. The director had his heart set on checking out one of the legendary Italian restaurants located on the Hill, and Heather was meeting her husband, Sonny, who was on the wrestling card at the Superstars of Wrestling match at the Arena. They agreed to meet, late in the evening at South Forty, a country and western dance bar.

Mitch kept telling Molly she was a worrywart. Telling her that he'd changed. She knew he hadn't, but finally gave in and agreed to drive into the city. She knew if she stayed in the trailer alone with him for much longer, she'd be lost.

She was certain that once they left the isolation of the movie set, Mitch would come to his senses and see her for the ordinary person she was. Not that she minded being ordinary. She liked who she was and planned to change for no one, give or take the last five of the ten pounds she was trying to lose.

No, once they were out in the real world Mitch would come to see they didn't have a future together. He'd admit to himself that what had happened between the two of them was nothing more than . . . circumstance.

The trip proved uneventful. On the one-hour drive they talked about the industry and the people in it. Mitch even revealed to her his dream of one day directing films, suggesting the two of them would make a great team. He could direct and she could produce.

Molly knew Mitch could do whatever he wanted, if he wanted it badly enough. He had talent in spades.

But she also knew if he didn't soon stabilize, he was going to be one of those shooting stars that burned out—the kind that have only one bright, shining moment and then are gone forever.

She couldn't stand by and watch that happen. Not after her brother, Joey. Loving someone was not enough to save them.

"I thought you were planning to join the others at the amusement park," Molly said, looking over her shoulder at the giant Ferris wheel partly visible above the treetops. They'd just sped past the entrance to Six Flags. "Don't you want to ride the Screaming Eagle roller coaster?"

"Nope. I prefer being with you."

Molly didn't know what to say to that, so she said nothing.

"I thought we'd find our own amusement," Mitch said. Glancing at her, he added, "However, if your thing is wild, screaming rides...I think I just might be able to accommodate you."

Ignoring his claim, she asked, "What exactly do you have planned, Mitch? Or should I be afraid to ask?"

"Pretty tame stuff, actually," he told her. "My brother Matthew had a girlfriend from Saint Louis once. He visited the city with her, and according to him, there were three places not to be missed. Of course, you've got to realize Matthew had this penchant for two things."

"What were they?"

"What else is there? Food and sex."

"I know I'll regret asking, but what are the three places?"

"Let's see. As I recall they were White Castle, Ted Drew's and ... ah ... Oh, I know. Moral Courts."

"Are you sure those aren't rap groups?" Molly asked doubtfully. She was pleased that Mitch could now talk about his brother, casually and with genuine fondness. Was he finally getting past the denial, anger and grief? She hoped so.

Mitch pointed. "That's a White Castle up ahead on the right." He pulled onto the parking lot of a burger joint shaped like a miniature castle and drove up to the drive-through speaker.

Turning to Molly before ordering he asked, "Burger, fries and Coke soft drink okay with you?"

"Mitch, I'm on a diet."

"Not tonight. Tonight all bets are off. It's cheap thrills all the way."

"Okay," Molly agreed with a sigh. Blowing her diet was probably the least damaging thing she could do tonight.

"Two dozen burgers, two fries and two large Coke drinks," Mitch ordered.

"Two dozen!"

"They're bite size. The locals call them sliders, 'cause they go down so easily. Unless you eat them at three in the morning, in which case they become belly bombers."

"At three in the morning everything becomes a belly bomber," Molly said dryly. "Not to worry. At three in the morning we're going to be safely tucked in, back at the movie location."

The delicious, oniony smell of the burgers permeated the car as they pulled out and into the traffic.

"Aren't we going to eat them now?" Molly asked. The aroma was making her mouth water.

"First we're going to pick up some concretes at Ted Drew's."

"Concretes?"

"Yeah, Ted Drew's is a frozen custard stand, specializing in frozen custard in a cup. Custard so thick you can turn it upside down and it won't fall out . . . hence the term 'concrete.'"

"And we're going to eat all this?"

"Sure, why not?"

"I hope one of those foil packets in your wallet is Alka-Seltzer."

Mitch just shot her a look and pulled onto Ted Drew's parking lot. "Where are we going to eat?" Molly asked as Mitch bought the local treat.

"Moral Courts. I hope they have a vibrating bed," Mitch answered, wiggling his eyebrows and handing her the custards to hold while he drove.

"What?"

"Don't look so innocent, Red. You're the one who wanted to go on an amusement ride."

"Moral Courts isn't a restaurant, then?" Molly swallowed dryly.

"According to Matthew it's this deliciously shady motel that has a wicked reputation for being a meeting place for lovers."

Lovers. She was helpless to resist. If she could control her emotions and just take what Mitch was offering, she would be able to walk away when the movie was over. Walk away whole instead of broken. Walk away with sweet memories.

And walk away with a secure future as an agent, because she'd saved Mitch Marlow from himself.

She couldn't fall in love with him. But try telling that to her heart!

Mitch pulled up their car in front of the motel office and parked right under the sign that said Vacancy and listed the hourly rate. Turning off the engine, he sort of slid down in the seat.

"What are you doing?" Molly asked, watching him in amazement.

"I'll wait here while you go inside and get us a key to the room. Okay?"

"You'll what? There's no way *I'm*—"

"You have to, Red." Reaching into the White Castle bag, he pulled out one of the tiny burgers and popped it into his mouth. "Think about it. I can't be the one to go inside and register us."

"Why not?"

Mitch took a drink of soda and swallowed. "What would your boss say, if my signature turned up on the register of Moral Courts while I was in your care? You're supposed to be baby-sitting me, keeping me out of trouble, remember? Not getting me into it."

"So don't sign your real name," Molly said, unconvinced.

"I'll still run the risk of being recognized. If that happens, there's a chance we'll find tabloid reporters camped outside our door when we try to leave. I think Peter would be even less thrilled with that."

"You've got so many good answers, you should be on 'Jeopardy,'" Molly grumbled.

"Now, Red, don't get testy," Mitch teased, reaching over and affectionately tugging a freewheeling, red curl. "I would have thought you, of all people, would be in favor of equal rights for women. After all, where is it written that the man is the one responsible for getting the room?"

"*Cosmo*," Molly answered blithely.

Holding out her hand, palm up, she added, "It's also written there that the man is the one who's responsible for paying for the room."

"Oh, I get it. You believe in equal rights for women only when it's convenient for women." The corner of his mouth lifted. "Aren't you ashamed of yourself, quibbling over money, when I've splurged on this delicious, gourmet repast for the two of us?"

"Okay, but what is Peter going to think when he sees this particular entry on my expense report?"

Mitch winced and reached for his wallet. "I should have known you'd win the round of 'Final Jeopardy,'" he said, handing her a stack of bills.

Molly returned a few minutes later with a key.

"See, now that wasn't so bad, was it?" Mitch said as he drove the car around to the side and parked it again.

"Actually, I have to admit that signing the motel register was quite a lot of fun," Molly told him, picking up the frozen custards while Mitch grabbed the sacks of burgers.

He was laughing as he balanced the food in one arm and unlocked the door to their motel room. "What did you do? Sign the register as Mr. and Mrs. John Smith?"

"No."

"What then?"

"Mr. and Mrs. Jesse Jerkface."

"You didn't!"

Molly nodded and collapsed onto the bed in giggles. Gaining control, she helped herself to a burger and cheese fry. "These are great, but they're going to add an inch to my hips," she moaned.

"Don't worry, Red," Mitch said, munching on a cheese fry. "I know of a way to burn up the calories and then some."

Molly glanced from him to the headboard. She was disappointed to see there wasn't a slot for quarters. So much for a vibrating bed.

"So do I," she countered, sampling the frozen custard and closing her eyes while it melted on her tongue.

"Okay, I'll bite," Mitch said, starting to work on his frozen custard, as well. His method was more voracious; he attacked his dessert, while Molly simply licked at hers. "So tell me. What do you want to do to burn up these calories we've just inhaled?"

"Go dancing."

"Dancing?"

Molly nodded.

"Now?" Mitch asked, his tone incredulous.

"No, later," she said mysteriously.

"Oh, good," he said, exhaling with relief.

"Now I want to go shopping."

"Shopping? You want to go shopping? Now?"

Molly put her empty custard cup aside and stood to stretch. "I think it would be fun to get together with everyone at South Forty, and I want to buy something fun to wear. Not that I ever need an excuse to go shopping."

"But we can't leave right now."

"Why not?"

"Because we've only been here ten minutes. I have a certain reputation to uphold."

"Yeah, but Jesse Jerkface doesn't," she reminded him.

"One condition." Mitch was hedging.

"What's that?"

"If we go shopping, I get to pick out the outfit."

"You pick it, you buy it," she told him.

"You're on."

Clearing the trash from their impromptu meal off the bed, they left the key on the dresser by the door. Mitch shook his head at the sight of the unrumpled bed, then they headed for the car. Opening the trunk, Mitch took out the white Stetson that was part of his costume in *Jesse*.

"My disguise," he explained, setting the Stetson low on his forehead and adding a pair of mirrored, aviator glasses. Fame could be a burden as well as a blessing, Molly realized abruptly. And anyone involved with Mitch Marlow would also have to pay the price of fame: lack of privacy.

Settling into the car, they headed south on one of the main arteries in search of a mall.

They found one within ten minutes. It was huge, sprawling over several acres.

In the first store they went into Molly tried on a short denim skirt and a red- and white-checked shirt.

Mitch shook his head.

Humoring him, she tried on a pair of jeans, a white blouse and a white leather vest.

"We'll take the vest," Mitch said, paying for it when she'd changed.

"I hope you know what you're doing," Molly commented. They looked for a shoe store. In the third one he found the pair of cowboy boots he wanted to buy for her.

They were bright red. They were exquisite, but they were bright red.

Red was not her color.

She quietly tried explaining that to Mitch, but to no avail. He pooh-poohed her argument that redheads did not wear the color red. Ever.

"These cowboy boots are three hundred dollars," she said, trying another tack.

Mitch just shrugged. "So I have good taste. Sue me."

"Expense and good taste are not necessarily the same thing," Molly retorted.

"She'll wear them," Mitch finally told the befuddled clerk.

"Mitch!"

"Humor me," he said over his shoulder as he paid for the boots.

Mitch took her arm possessively when they left the store, and Molly began to feel that people in the crowded mall were staring. She wasn't sure whether they were looking at the two of them or her red, cowboy boots. *Silly goose,* she told herself. They're looking at Mitch, of course.

No one in the crowd recognized him, though he looked drop-dead gorgeous in his faded, sleeveless, chambray shirt, jeans and black, silver-trimmed belt above the hard, flat belly. The white Stetson and mirrored sunglasses only added to his allure of mystery.

Molly looked again at her red boots, then back at Mitch. "Can I ask you a question?"

"Sure."

"Do you know what you're doing?"

"Of course. I love to shop. Maybe not as much as I'd have loved to stay at Moral Courts with you, but hey, I'm a new man! You've done exactly what Peter asked you to do. You've created a new and improved..." he paused and whispered "...Mitch Marlow."

"Then I can safely assume the outfit you have in mind consists of more than a white leather vest and red leather, cowboy boots?"

"Indeed. We need two more items to complete the outfit I have in mind. Just trust me."

In the next store he urged her to try on a pair of jean shorts.

"I can't wear these."

"Try them," he urged.

She put them on reluctantly.

"Great. We'll take them. Wrap them up."

"Are you sure?" Molly asked, thinking about thighs that weren't perfect.

"Sure. Don't you like them?" Mitch asked, not seeming to understand.

"They're fine," she said, suddenly feeling very good.

"One last purchase and we're finished," Mitch said, adding the package to the others. He checked his watch. "We've got a half hour till everyone's meeting at South Forty."

"Let's just get the white blouse I tried the vest on with," Molly suggested.

Mitch shook his head. "No blouse."

"No blouse?"

"I think it's sexy when you button it and wear it by itself."

"Then we can leave," Molly said, though she wasn't altogether certain about the vest idea.

"We still have something to buy to complete the outfit," Mitch insisted.

"What?"

"Come along," he said, taking her hand and leading her to Victoria's Secret.

"I don't think they allow men in here," Molly said, hanging back.

"Will you come on," he said, tugging her inside.

Surrounded by all the lace and silks displayed in the store, he looked even more virile.

"Can I help you?"

The salesclerk didn't even acknowledge Molly's presence. She was completely focused on Mitch. Molly wanted to smack her. She was feeling very possessive and wondered where the feeling had come from.

"We'd like to see what you have in thigh-high stockings," she heard Mitch say.

Before Molly could collect herself to object, the salesgirl was back with samples.

Mitch glanced over the flat, narrow boxes and picked out one. "We'll take these."

Molly continued to watch, openmouthed, as he handed the salesgirl a pair of white, bow-patterned lace, thigh-high stockings.

"Stockings go under something, Mitch," Molly insisted. "Jean shorts and cowboy boots don't allow for that."

"The stockings are great," Mitch maintained as they rode down the escalator. "I want you to go into the ladies' room and change into everything. When you see it all on together, you'll realize it's a great look for you."

"I don't know, Mitch."

"I do," he said. "Go ahead and try everything on. I'll wait for you out here."

Full of misgiving, Molly went inside. If she didn't like the outfit, she didn't have to come out of the ladies' room, she decided.

Two girls were putting on makeup and spraying their hair. "That is so hot!" they said when Molly walked out of one of the stalls.

"You don't think it's a little too—?"

"No," the two girls said in unison. One of them asked where she'd gotten the stockings, and they went out, chattering about wearing the same look with their cowboy boots, leaving a trail of hair spray behind them.

"Well, I guess if it plays in the Midwest..." Molly said to her reflection in the mirror. She did look very feminine . . . and very sexy. Madonna would be proud of her.

Picking up her shopping bag, she went out to submit to Mitch's inspection, suddenly feeling like a girlfriend. She was getting into dangerous waters and didn't seem to be able to swim to the shallow end of the pool.

The appreciative grin on Mitch's face when he saw her reinforced her confidence.

"Didn't I tell you how great you'd look?" he said, taking her arm.

"Mitch, people are gawking," she whispered, secretly enjoying the moment.

"'Cause you look so hot," he whispered, nibbling at her ear.

"Don't be ridiculous. They're looking at you, Mitch. You're the celebrity."

"They don't know that. But they do know you look hot, baby. I'm getting you out of here, before some young stud decides he can take my woman."

Sweeping her up, he proceeded to do just that.

"Mitch, will you please put me down!" she demanded, hiding her face. "You're making a spectacle."

"Don't worry about it, Red. Just enjoy being swept off your feet," he teased.

"You can't carry me to the car! I'm too heavy."

"Boy, you must have been dating some weak Nellies. You're a handful, but I like having my hands full. Just hang on and enjoy the ride, Red."

"Mitch!"

"Shut up or I'll kiss you."

"Mitch!"

"I warned you," he said. His lips came down to meet hers.

It seemed to take forever, but finally they were at the car. He set her down then and opened the door.

Molly felt dazed as they pulled out and into the traffic. She'd never been romanced quite like this. Mitch didn't do anything by halves. But only a lunatic would fall in love with a Hollywood heartthrob.

"How far is South Forty?" Molly asked, suddenly in the mood to dance. To do anything but be alone with Mitch.

"Maybe ten minutes."

"Which way are we going?"

"The long way."

"Why?"

"Because I want to make a stop along the way."

"Oh." She didn't ask why, figuring he wanted to sneak a cigarette in a men's room or something. She could hardly complain, after the way she'd blown her diet.

Five minutes later he pulled back into Moral Courts. This time he rented the room. Seconds later he was back in the car with the key.

"What's going on?" she asked, knowing the answer perfectly well.

"You wanted to dance, right?"

Molly nodded.

"Well, I'd be much too uncomfortable to dance in my current condition," he explained, letting her into the room.

"Mitch . . ."

"Shut up and kiss me, Red," he said, kicking the door shut with one booted foot and pulling her into his possessive embrace.

His kiss was hungry with need.

When she responded with equal fire, his arms tightened, bringing her closer still. His hips ground against hers and he shuddered.

"I thought we'd never get here," he said, drawing a breath, then holding her away from him for a slow, leisurely perusal.

"You like the outfit, I take it," Molly said, posing for effect, luxuriating in the way he made her feel.

"I like the woman in the outfit," he vowed, his voice a raspy drawl. He pulled her back to him and took possession of her mouth once again.

Deepening the kiss, he unzipped her jean shorts, slid in his hand to cup her, then slipped his finger inside.

Pleasure rippled through Molly. He almost brought her to orgasm while he kissed her senseless, caressing her without stopping.

She was breathing shallowly and could barely see when he unzipped his own jeans after she'd unbuckled his belt.

"Touch me, Red," he whispered.

Her hand freed his blatantly hard desire, her fingers circling the throbbing, while he cupped his hands over her buttocks, squeezing, rhythmically kneading.

"I have to have you...now!" he cried with a low moan. Pulling down her shorts, he dropped to his knees, covering her with a sucking kiss.

Just as her knees were about to buckle, he pulled her down to straddle him, thrusting into her waiting, moist acceptance.

Molly arched to meet him, and their raging passion slammed into a body-quaking, mutual orgasm.

The room was silent but for their ragged breathing.

Mitch rested his head in Molly's riotous red curls.

"Good golly, Miss Molly..." he said with wonderment. They collapsed onto the floor, weak, sated and healed. Neither would ever be the same again.

Mitch lifted Molly's hand to his lips, kissed her palm and sighed happily.

Molly broke the silence.

"I have to know something, Mitch," she said, her tone serious.

"Anything, Red...anything at all."

"How did you sign the register?"

"What?"

"How did you sign the register when you got the key for the room?" Molly repeated.

"Are you sure you want to know?"

"Yes," she said, propping her head on one hand.

A wicked grin preceded Mitch's answer.

"Mr. and Mrs. Peter Ketteridge."

11

SOUTH FORTY'S parking lot was jam-packed.

The scattered couples Molly and Mitch passed on their way in paid them little heed. They were lost in their own flirtations.

Mitch pulled his white Stetson low as they approached the dance hall. He paid the entry fee, and they were getting their hands stamped when Heather came storming out, a glowering Sonny Simms not far behind her.

She brushed past without a word. They heard her scream something derogatory at him. Moments later Sonny returned, without Heather.

"To hell with her," he said. "Let her leave. I don't need her prissy ass telling me what to do."

Mitch raised his eyebrows above his sunglasses, but said nothing; the two of them made their way across the cavernous room toward an empty table. A waitress came up and took their orders and they settled back to watch the crowd, looking for familiar faces.

The evening was in full swing, with experienced performers circle dancing the country two-step on the outer edge, and less experienced dancers doing whatever they could in the center of the floor.

Mitch noticed a corner had been made into a shop that sold cowboy boots, hats and jeans. Country gear was, in fact, the clothing of choice. Everyone was dressed in some version of Western cool, though no one looked as sexy as his Molly.

She'd simply knocked him silly. Now he could even empathize with Sonny Simms. Having it bad for a woman was the scariest thing on earth.

The waitress returned with their beers and an order of buffalo wings for the next table. He couldn't believe he was hungry again. Did being in love make you hungry? He didn't know. He'd certainly never felt like this before.

"So you two decided to have some fun, after all, did you?" Angie said, coming up to the table with the key grip in tow. She picked up Molly's beer and took a sip. "Come join us on the dance floor," she shouted, pulling her partner along with her.

"Let's boogie," Mitch said, standing and offering Molly his hand.

He knew she was glad the place was packed. No matter how often he assured her the outfit he'd bought her was fine, he knew she still felt self-conscious. How ridiculous, when she was the sexiest thing he'd ever seen! All that red hair and curves meant danger. Said woman.

He pulled her into his arms for a slow dance, even though the music wasn't slow. The band was playing a Dwight Yoakam tune about living wild and dangerously. He certainly was doing just that, but Molly would see to it that the film was finished without any more crises, and then she'd be gone.

To her he was just a job. The attraction between them was only a fringe benefit.

He cupped his hand on the back of her neck, beneath her long tresses, and pulled her close for a sweet and lazy kiss. *God, woman, what are you doing to me?* he thought. He couldn't let himself love again. Losing hurt too much.

He couldn't even make any promises. There was nothing less secure than an actor's life.

Someone tapped him on the shoulder. It was Sonny—if a man as big as Sonny could tap—it felt more like a shove.

"Go away," Mitch said, shrugging off the intrusive hand.

"I'm cutting in."

"No," Mitch said.

It was obvious that Sonny was spoiling for a fight. Well, he'd come to the right place. Filled with frustration, Mitch would be only too happy to oblige him.

Big as a mountain, he'd make an easy target.

"I'll dance with him," Molly said.

"No, you won't," Mitch declared, holding her tight; Molly wouldn't like him fighting.

"Let the little lady make up her own mind. Maybe she'd rather dance with a real man instead of some candy-ass actor like you."

"Shut up," Mitch warned; people were starting to take an interest in their altercation. "Go find Heather and make up. Leave us alone."

"Heather doesn't want to make up. All I hear from her is, 'Why can't you be more like Mitch?' Maybe we should just change partners. I'll dance with Molly and you can go find Heather."

"You're causing a scene," Mitch pointed out, trying to maneuver away from the angry wrestler.

"I don't care. And don't you be talking down to me, boy. I'm just as big a star as you are. And I earned my star status in the ring, with real men. I'm not just some pretty boy."

"You can say that again," Mitch grumbled beneath his breath.

"What was that?" Sonny demanded. He was plainly looking for any excuse to turn their disagreement into a full-fledged fight.

"I said there are lots of women here who'd be happy to dance with a superstar like you. Why don't you go ask one of them? Let it be, man."

"Who do you think you are? Friggin' Paul McCartney?" Sonny asked, enraged. The growing crowd encouraging him to make an open challenge, Sonny was either going to dance with Molly or fight with him.

"Come on, Mitch," Molly whispered, trying to free her hand. "I'll dance with him once and he'll be satisfied. Don't let him push you into doing something foolish. It's only one dance."

"You're not dancing with him," Mitch insisted. "This isn't about dancing. He wants a shot at me because of Heather. He's got it into his head that there was something between us, when there wasn't."

"I'm losing patience," Sonny said. "Is she going to dance with me or not?"

"Not."

"Oh, hell. She's not in Heather's league, anyway," Sonny snarled.

Mitch let go Molly's hand and decked Sonny with a punch he couldn't have seen coming. "That's right, she's way out of Heather's league, you bastard," Mitch said, standing over him.

The crowd fell silent when Sonny got up and staggered toward Mitch.

No one paid much attention to the cameraman who edged forward to snap photographs of the brawl that ensued.

MITCH LAY SPRAWLED on the sofa in the trailer. "How do you feel?" Molly asked, handing him an ice pack.

"Like I moved a mountain," he groaned.

"More like the mountain moved you."

"You can say that again. That guy felt like a freight train when he hit me."

"You need to grow up, you know that. It's time you stopped using your brother's death as an excuse for your wild and reckless behavior. It's long past time you took responsibility for your own actions."

"Molly, my head hurts. Don't yell."

"I'll yell if I want to. And you, the next time you look in the mirror at that handsome face of yours, take a real good look. You're being nothing but a scared adolescent, if you'd rather be dead than grow up. If you're successful, it doesn't take anything away from Matthew."

"But . . . Molly, I was only trying to protect you. I didn't mean to start a fight, honest, I didn't."

"I could have protected myself. Your starting the fight last night was a cop-out—little-boy stuff. And frankly, I don't have time for little boys."

The telephone rang.

"Hello," Molly said in a surly tone.

"Is Mitch alive? I hope so, so I can kill him."

"Yes, Peter, he's alive."

"Is he in any shape for filming?"

"No, he won't be in any shape to go before the cameras until his face heals . . . it could take days. Yes, I know how much that is going to cost the studio."

"I sent you there to make sure something like this didn't happen."

"I know I'm responsible," Molly agreed.

"Tell him it was my fault," Mitch said.

"You want to talk to Mitch?" Molly asked Peter, only too happy to hand over.

"No. I want to talk to you."

"Me?" she said, resigned to hearing the worst.

Molly rubbed her eyes. She had hardly slept at all during the night. She'd been up, nursing Mitch's cuts and bruises. She didn't want to talk to Peter. He didn't sound as if he was in a very happy mood.

"This is just what I needed this morning, when I can't even move," Peter growled.

"What do you mean, you can't move?" Molly asked, looking at the receiver, puzzled. Had she heard aright?

"I reached for a newspaper and threw my back out," Peter explained. "Have you seen the morning edition of the *International Intruder?*"

"No, I haven't. Why?"

Peter told her with quiet fury.

"No!" she cried.

"What?" Mitch asked with a groan. "What is it?"

"I don't believe it," Molly said when Peter repeated the news.

"What?" Mitch asked again, wincing this time.

"You're fired, Ms. Hill."

"I understand, sir," Molly said. She hung up.

"What?" Mitch persisted, sitting up with a great deal of agony.

"You'll be happy to hear you finally accomplished what you wanted to do since I got here."

"What are you talking about?"

"Peter just fired me."

"He did what? Why?"

"Seems the two of us made the cover of the *International Intruder.*"

12

"YOU WAKE HIM UP," Angie told the key grip when he asked why Mitch wasn't on the set.

"Not me, but the director is madder'n hell. Somebody better wake him up. It's the last scene—then we can go home." He looked at Angie expectantly.

"Okay, I'll do it, since you put it that way," Angie agreed. Being around Mitch for the last few days was about as much fun as a dance without a punch bowl to spike. The whole crew had been walking on eggs ever since Molly's departure.

"I'm here," Mitch growled, coming out of his trailer. "Let's get this over. I've got business in Hollywood to get to. Important business."

"Her name wouldn't be Molly Hill, would it?" Angie said, dripping sarcasm.

"Angie, you're a woman," Mitch said, then paused.

"You got great powers of observation there, Marlow."

"What I mean is, maybe you can tell me why Molly won't return my calls."

"I'm sure I don't know, you being such a charming fellow and all," Angie replied, no less sarcastically.

"So I was stupid."

"So you were."

"You've never done anything stupid?"

"Not on such a regular basis. It's like you're getting college credit for it. You must be approaching your master's degree in bad moves."

"So give me some help here. What can I do to get her to take my calls?"

"Nothing."

"You're a lot of help."

"Mitch, reaching out and touching someone is always better done in person."

"You think she'll see me then?"

"No."

"What?"

"Not at first, but if you love her, you'll find a way to make her see it."

Mitch nodded.

"You do love her, don't you?" Angie persisted, ever the pesky younger sister.

"I don't know. I've never been in love. I didn't expect to miss her like this."

"Well, find a way to figure it out and make things right."

Mitch walked onto the set to play his last scene and vowed to do just that. Molly had been right about him. He had been self-indulgent. His guilt and suicidal behavior would not negate Matthew's death. It would only dishonor his brother.

It was time to grow up—at the very least, time to apologize to Molly. Time to accept the responsibility of life.

If, indeed, it was Molly he wanted. He had to find out. Happiness could be snatched away in a heartbeat, as it had been when Matthew died.

Did he love her?

Did she love him?

He had to find out.

MOLLY SAT ALONE in her apartment.

Her bags were still sitting in a corner, unpacked. She didn't see any reason why she should unpack them, when she couldn't unpack her heart.

It was still in the Midwest with Mitch Marlow.

The scum.

The snake.

The most wonderful, impossible man she'd ever met.

She hated him.

She loved him.

She was crying again.

And, oh, hell! She was out of tissues.

MOLLY LAY in the soft cocoon of her bed.

"I'm No Angel" was playing once again on the tape deck. Yes, Mitch had taken her to places she'd never been when she'd gone for a ride with him.

She'd lost him and her heart. She had only to look at the cover of the *International Intruder*—the one with the picture of Mitch and Sonny fighting over her. The black-and-white photograph was a record of the outfit Mitch had bought her, a record of her failure.

Her dream of becoming an agent had been destroyed. No one would hire her now. She'd not only failed at what Peter had sent her to do; she'd been made to look a perfect fool by a tabloid photographer who'd been following the battling Simms.

The movie poster on the back of her closet door was from *Dangerous*. She hadn't taken it down. Instead she'd drawn a red circle with a slash through it. Drawing it had been very satisfying.

Oh, hell! She was crying again.

And now she was out of toilet tissue.

MOLLY AWOKE from a deep sleep, her fogged brain pounding. She shook her head but the fog didn't go away.

Someone was pounding on the door.

She blinked twice and looked at the clock on her bedside table. It was six in the morning. Who would come to her apartment at six in the morning?

Throwing on a robe, she yawned, fumbled to tie the sash and made her way to the door.

"Who is it?" she called out.

Her heart sank when she heard the voice.

Mitch!

Suddenly she was awake and fully alert. What was he doing here? Hadn't he already gotten what he wanted?

He hadn't tried to stop her leaving.

Sure, there had been phone calls, but they'd only been made to assuage the guilt he felt over getting her fired. She didn't really think he'd planned that.

Hell, he hadn't made any plans at all.

And she'd made way too many. Too many foolish plans.

"Go away," she called through the door. She couldn't let him in. She couldn't let him see how devastated she'd been by the ending of their affair.

"Molly, let me in. We need to talk."

"We have nothing to say to each other," she said, leaning her forehead against the door. If he'd had something to say—something she'd wanted to hear—he would have said it before she left the movie location. He wouldn't have let her leave.

"Come on, Red," he persisted. "Let me in," knocking loudly enough to wake her neighbors.

"Go away. You're going to wake the neighborhood."

"Look, I know we can work this out if you'll just let me in."

"I don't want to see you." That was a lie. She was dying to see him. God, how she'd missed seeing him.

"Stop being so damn stubborn. Let me in, Molly. I need to talk to you."

"I'm not your agent any longer. I'm not anyone's agent. Talk to Peter."

"Aw, Molly, will you stop? Everything just got all messed up. I didn't mean—"

"Funny how that always happens when you're involved, isn't it, Mitch? You never think about how what you do affects other people."

"Molly, I'm sorry. I want you to understand how sorry I am."

"I understand. You're sorry. Now will you go away?"

"You're not going to let me in, are you?" Mitch said. She heard a groan of frustration.

"No."

"*Molly!*"

"Go away. Just . . . just go."

"You're being . . . you're being impossible. I could just . . ."

"You could just leave."

"You really aren't going to let me in?"

"You catch on slowly . . . but you do catch on."
He was so used to getting his way with women that she could hear the genuine disbelief in his voice.

"Okay, I'm leaving."

"Goodbye."

"Molly . . ."

"Go."

MOLLY SAT AROUND the apartment all day, watching the soaps. She read all the trade news journals and did her nails twice.

She didn't dare leave the house, because she was afraid she'd find Mitch sitting in her hallway, lying in wait. It hadn't sounded as if he'd gotten the message.

If only she could believe her own words! She'd told him to leave, but she'd wanted to let him in. She still wanted to be with him. There was no hope for her.

She hadn't called her parents yet, but it was on the agenda. She'd call them in a day or two. Maybe by then she would have figured out if there was any way at all to salvage the mess she'd gotten herself into.

Tomorrow. Like Scarlett, she'd pull herself together tomorrow.

MITCH WALKED BAREFOOT along the beach in the moonlight. He'd neither slept nor shaved, his clothes were rumpled.

Who would have thought it? Molly Hill. She wasn't what he'd been looking for. He hadn't really been looking for a woman. But she'd turned out to be just what he needed.

But he'd been too dumb to see it. He'd let her just walk away—no, he'd pushed her.

He had to get her back. He had to.

Falling to his knees in the sand, he rubbed his sleep-weary eyes. "I love her . . . I just didn't know. You've got to help me get her back, Matthew," he said to the wind that blew a page of newsprint into his face.

MOLLY SLEPT LATE the following morning.

When she finally awoke, she felt as if she were fighting her way out of a marshmallow. Days of self-indulgence lay blurred in her memory, blended with nights of romantic, erotic dreams.

Mitch Marlow might not be pounding on her door, but thoughts of him wouldn't leave her alone.

She had to get out of the apartment today. Yesterday she'd been afraid to leave, afraid she'd find Mitch camped on her doorstep.

Looking into the refrigerator, she saw that she was out of everything without fuzz on it. It was definitely time to go to the market. Besides, her crying jags had left her without tissue of any kind.

Maybe if she got dressed and went out she'd gain some perspective. After all, Peter Ketteridge didn't own the only talent agency in L.A. Maybe she could start again, smaller, lower down in the pecking order.

Maybe she could start her own agency.

Yeah, right. And *International Intruder* reporters got up before the sun went down.

Throwing on some clothes, she paused to check her appearance in the mirror she'd been avoiding. She shrugged.

In her baggy jeans, oversize sweater and ponytail, the only fashion statement she was making was a 911 call to the fashion police.

Grabbing her canvas bag, she headed out the door after a careful inspection of the hallway for any loitering movie stars. She knew she was being ridiculous. Mitch's visit yesterday had only been made out of some sense of duty—or worse, pity. He had probably already moved on, to Heather or a Heather clone.

The market was half-empty, making shopping less of an obstacle course than usual. The first aisle yielded up microwave popcorn, one of the staples of singles. Aisle two brought her a case of Diet Coke drinks.... She now had seven pounds to lose instead of five. Aisle three had tissues. She picked up ten boxes although she absolutely, positively was not going to cry again for at least a week.

Aisles five and six offered frozen pizza and romance novels; after all, somewhere there had to be a happy ending and a hot meal. In aisle seven she found DoveBar ice creams, in case she felt faint from all the crying.

She was almost surprised that no one paid her the least attention. Hadn't she been on the cover of the *International Intruder?*

There was a line at the checkout counter. If there were only two people in the store, there was a line at the checkout counter. It was written in Murphy's Law. In ink.

The lady in front of her had a two-year-old toddler in her cart. Molly wondered what aisle the lady had found her in. Maybe a toddler was what *she* needed. A child would certainly make her less self-absorbed. Being self-absorbed wasn't what it was cracked up to be, when the self involved was boring.

What would Mitch's child—their child—look like? She started crying.

She was being stupid, stupid, stupid, she muttered, pulling tissue from one of the boxes she'd thrown into her cart. She tried smiling at the toddler, but he just threw his troll doll at her. And laughed.

Men, she muttered, bending to retrieve the doll. On her way up, her eyes caught sight of the *International Intruder* for the first time.

Oh, my God!

The headline left her speechless.

Quickly handing the toddler back his doll, she reached into her bag for her sunglasses and slid them on. She felt herself blanch as she reread the words that screamed at her from the tabloid.

She was going to kill him.

Mitch Marlow was dead meat.

But first she had to get rid of the tabloids. Gathering them up, she dumped them into the cart with everything else. The clerk looked at her a little oddly, but rang them up with her groceries without comment, then gave her the total in a bored monotone.

Molly paid her tab and fled with the evidence, as if it were the loot from some bank job. On the way home she looked neither right nor left, just straight ahead, as if she were wearing blinders. She kept going, one foot in front of the other, heading for the safety of her own apartment.

There was no safety to be found there.

A throng of reporters and photographers was camped outside, swarming around the place like bees. If they saw her, she'd be stung. She had to slip away before that happened.

What was she going to do?

She was trapped.

Trapped with melting groceries and an armful of the *International Intruder*.

She looked down at the bold headline and still couldn't believe her eyes: Molly Hill . . . Will You Marry Me? . . . Mitch Marlow.

The scum.

The snake.

The . . . the . . . She had to think quickly. Where could she go?

And then it came to her. Of course. The person who was responsible for her getting into this mess in the first place.

Peter Ketteridge.

She'd go to his office.

What could he do—fire her?

PETER'S GREETING was effusive and unexpected.

"It's about time you came back to work," he said, taking her things and ushering her in. "Where have you been?"

"You fired me," Molly said.

"Silly girl. I'm always firing someone. No one takes it seriously. Besides, your campaign to reverse Mitch's image is simply brilliant."

"My campaign?"

Peter held up a copy of the *International Intruder*, thumping the headline, marriage proposal.

"Yes, this is brilliant. I can't believe I didn't think of it myself. All the world loves a good romance."

"But it wasn't my idea—there is no—I don't—"

A commotion in the outside lobby drowned Molly's stammered objection. She sucked in a quick, startled breath when she saw Mitch. He was followed by a gaggle of shoving reporters and photographers. Shouldering his way into Peter's office, Mitch joined them.

"You've seen the morning paper," Mitch said, nodding to the stack on Peter's desk. "Are you collecting them for souvenirs, Molly?"

She glared at him.

"Well, Red," he continued calmly, "we're all waiting for your answer."

All at once Molly saw past the self-assured movie star to the scared man who had risked the ultimate humiliation to win her heart, to prove that he loved her.

She couldn't say no.

But she could make him squirm. And she would enjoy every delicious moment of the torture.

"I don't see anyone on bended knee." She sniffed, pushing back her curls.

"Now you do," he answered, dropping onto one knee. Cameras flashed.

"Peter's rehired me," she said, taking care to put her boss on record next. "Do I have to quit my job, if we get married?" she asked him.

"No," Peter answered.

Molly looked to Mitch for confirmation. "You heard the boss," he said and shrugged. "But there is one condition."

"And what might that be?"

"I have to be your number one client."

"I think that can be arranged. Right, Peter?"

Peter nodded.

She stalled. "Will you still give me extravagant clothing?"

"As much as your mercenary heart desires," he teased, "on one condition."

"What's that?" she asked warily.

"Anything I pay for, I get to pick out," he answered.

Molly felt her face flame, but went on. "One last thing."

"One last thing," Mitch agreed.

"I get to choose all your leading ladies."

"Done."

"Do you promise?"

"Red . . ."

"What?"

"Shut up and say yes."

"Yes."

13

International Intruder

Dateline L.A.

She Said Yes!

It wasn't easy. He had to do it on bended knee, but Hollywood heartthrob, Mitch Marlow, convinced his agent, Molly Hill, to marry him. That's a long way to go not to have to pay your ten percent, Marlow.

Stay tuned for wedding pics. You know the *Intruder* will get them.

International Intruder

Dateline L.A.

Jesse Is Taking the Loot!

Mitch Marlow has a monster hit on his hands and his new movie, *Jesse*, isn't even out yet. The trailer being previewed in movie theaters around the country has shot Marlow's ballad from *Jesse* to number one on the pop charts and created unprecedented interest in an unreleased movie.

Of course, the *Intruder* will be there for the premiere.

International Intruder

Dateline L.A.

Jesse Steals the Gold!

Two thumbs up. Five stars. *Jesse* has heart and Hollywood heartthrob, Mitch Marlow, in chaps and spurs. The former is going to win the film an Oscar nomination, and the latter is raking in more gold at the box office than Jesse James ever dreamed of.

We were there for the star-studded premiere, and the *Intruder* will be there for the Oscar awards.

International Intruder

Dateline L.A.

Elvis Spotted At Hollywood Wedding!

Superagent Molly Hill wed Oscar nominee Mitch Marlow in the garden of Peter Ketteridge's Beverly Hills mansion.

The bride and groom slipped briefly into a white canvas tent before the wedding for some sort of private ceremony.

But they weren't missed by the wedding guests, who were busy gawking at Elvis, filling his tuxedo pockets with wedding cake.

The *Intruder*'s film didn't develop. Could it be that Elvis is a vampire?

International Intruder

Dateline L.A.

Molly Marlow Steals Oscar Spotlight!

Mitch Marlow won the Oscar for his portrayal of Jesse James in *Jesse*, but his very pregnant wife stole the show by going into labor during his acceptance speech.

The *Intruder* will have first pictures of the Marlow heir.

International Intruder

Dateline L.A.

It's a Boy! It's a Boy!

It's twins! Matthew and Peter Marlow were born at midnight and one minute after.

Mitch is rumored to have given Molly a string of antique pearls. Molly, the nurses on the maternity floor claim, gave Mitch a certificate for a vasectomy.

The *Intruder* doesn't believe it for a moment. There are sure to be more productions coming from this talented team.

International Intruder

Dateline L.A.

The Ketteridge Agency Goes Coed!

Molly Marlow has become a full-fledged partner with Peter Ketteridge. The first project of the new Ketteridge Marlow Agency is a film to be directed by Molly's Oscar-winning husband, Mitch Marlow.

The film is to star Sonny and Heather Simms as Beauty and the Beast, the nineties version.

This is one the *Intruder* wants to watch!

International Intruder

Dateline L.A.

Who Is This Mystery Woman?

Is Peter Ketteridge about to sprinkle fairy dust upon the lovely who appeared with him on the "Run Away with the Rich and Famous" segment, or were the six hulking men in the background indicative of a more personal interest?

Anyone who can identify this mystery woman will win a year's free subscription to the *Intruder*.

International Intruder

Dateline L.A.

Confirmed Bachelor Bites the Dust!

Mrs. Thelma Ketteridge of L.A. announced the engagement of her only son, Peter Ketteridge, to Angie Weir, the mystery woman who accompanied him on the Life-styles trip.

Angie's six older brothers were seen emerging from the Ketteridge Marlow Agency last week, no doubt there to congratulate Peter on his wise decision to marry their baby sister.

A free subscription to the *International Intruder* is going out to Mrs. Thelma Ketteridge.

Epilogue

"HOW DO YOU SUPPOSE Peter and Angie are handling the weekend with the twins?" Mitch asked Molly as they entered their room at Moral Courts, White Castle burgers and Ted Drew's concretes in hand.

"They've probably taken a vow of childlessness," Molly said and laughed.

"And doglessness," Mitch added, referring to the pair of Irish setter puppies they'd bought the twins.

"How did you register this time?" Molly asked, plopping onto the bed and unwrapping one of the bite-size burgers.

"Mr. and Mrs. Mitch Marlow," he said proudly.

"Do you think that's wise?" she asked.

"Are you kidding? I've also arranged for them to put up a plaque in this room."

"What?" Molly asked, choking.

"If Michael Jackson can have his own room at Disneyland . . ."

They took turns feeding each other between laughter and kisses. Sweet memories of another time shared the room with them.

"Well, what do you want to do now, Mrs. Marlow?" Mitch asked when they'd polished off the last of the food.

Molly considered him as he leaned against the headboard, hands clasped behind his head. Her eyes shone.

"Shopping is a good way to celebrate an anniversary," she suggested.

He shook his head.

"Dancing is another good way to celebrate."

He shook his head.

"No shopping? No dancing? Is that what you're saying?"

"You catch on fast, Red. We can't leave the room right now."

"Why not?"

"We've only been here ten minutes. I have a reputation to uphold as a Hollywood heartthrob. I signed my real name at the register, remember."

"I see," Molly said, crawling up the bed to lie across him. She turned off the light.

He unzipped her linen walking shorts. "Did you bring the red cowboy boots?" he asked.

Molly laughed again. "You've got a fetish, Mr. Marlow."

"Yeah," he agreed, tugging at her soft, springy curls. "I love the color red."

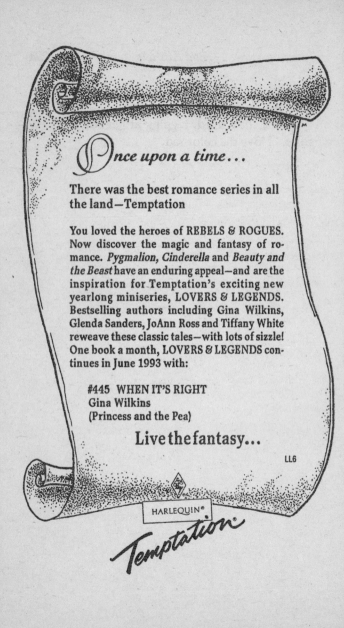

Relive the romance...
Harlequin and Silhouette
are proud to present

by Request

A program of collections of three complete novels by the most requested authors with the most requested themes. Be sure to look for one volume each month with three complete novels by top name authors.

In June: **NINE MONTHS** Penny Jordan
Stella Cameron
Janice Kaiser

Three women pregnant and alone. But a lot can happen in nine months!

In July: **DADDY'S HOME** Kristin James
Naomi Horton
Mary Lynn Baxter

Daddy's Home... and his presence is long overdue!

In August: **FORGOTTEN PAST** Barbara Kaye
Pamela Browning
Nancy Martin

Do you dare to create a future if you've forgotten the past?

Available at your favorite retail outlet.